# TERESA'S TREASURE

Teresa, as a child, dreamt of the day, when the secret inside a tin box would be revealed to her. However, as she grows into a young woman her life changes dramatically, shattering her childhood dreams . . . yet she still remembers her treasure. Risking a possible marriage match, Teresa decides to go on a journey of discovery to seek it out. But some secrets are meant to stay buried. What she discovers is of greater value than she had ever imagined.

VALERIE HOLMES

# TERESA'S TREASURE

*Complete and Unabridged*

**LINFORD**
*Leicester*

First published in Great Britain in 2012

First Linford Edition
published 2012

British Library CIP Data

Holmes, Valerie.
 Teresa's treasure. - -
 (Linford romance library)
 1. Love stories.
 2. Large type books.
 I. Title II. Series
 823.9′2–dc23

 ISBN 978–1–4448–1144–5

Published by
F. A. Thorpe (Publishing)
Anstey, Leicestershire

Set by Words & Graphics Ltd.
Anstey, Leicestershire
Printed and bound in Great Britain by
T. J. International Ltd., Padstow, Cornwall

This book is printed on acid-free paper

# The Prologue

Joe was bent double over the end of the unhinged scullery door, which was propped upside down against a low table. He was squinting hard to avoid the splinters flying into his eyes as he worked on the old hard wood, smoothing it down with a heavy plane. The door no longer closed after the heavy winter rain. He stopped as a shadow blocked out his light, making it impossible for him to see what he was doing.

Glancing up at the small figure of the eleven year old daughter of the house, who was staring at him anxiously, he smiled. The sunlight seemed to add an extra glow to her voluminous ash blonde curls, bringing out a faint auburn hint amidst its mass. Joe had no doubt that she was going to grow into a woman any man would be proud of, only too soon. Her pretty apple green slippers were getting a covering of dust and sand as she sidestepped in her excited state.

Joe paused for a moment and stopped his work. 'Now, what would bring you all the way out here on your own, lass? Your pretty green dress and those pumps are not meant for Joe's workhouse is they now?' He smiled at her through tired eyes, his grizzled face was rough but kindly, but Joe soon realised that all was not well as he could see that she was very agitated, stepping from one foot to the other as she stared at him. 'What is it, Miss Teresa?' he asked, speaking softly in his gruff voice. Her slight figure blocked the autumnal light as she hovered in the doorway, nervously looking around her.

Teresa was edging inside the scullery, watchful that she was not seen by Mrs Shellow, the housekeeper from the manor farm house, who would be carrying out her duties in the adjoining building.

Joe Lampton put down the plane he had been using to shave the bottom of the swollen door so that it would close once more, and instead gave all his attention to the young miss. 'Has something happened in the house, Miss Teresa?' He knew she was a sensitive child and did not want to alarm her further. Joe also knew that lass would soon have enough to worry about; perhaps they had told her already.

'No, well, yes, but not something bad, not this time, that is. You see I have something very special . . . to hide.' Teresa stepped down into the work room that was at the back of the scullery, her shoes stepping further onto the sandy floor. The room's open door faced towards the seaside where a vast sweeping beach of fine sand lined the shoreline, touching the German sea, as white crested waves crashed ashore. The small stable block, which housed the carriage horses, was the only building which stood between the building and the open beach. The fishermen's cottages nestled to its side. Alunby was a ramshackle sort of place that had been added to as and when needed by the villagers and the owners of Marsh Farm estate. The wild dunes and sea provided the only barrier for the sand that seemed to get inside everywhere, carried on the frequent winds from across the sea that would whip it up.

Joe looked at the girl. She was dressed impeccably in a dress edged with real cream lace, the emerald ribbons contrasting with her sandy curls and trimming her outfit to perfection, to match the bows of her slippers. Her outfits were always chosen carefully by her mama. This was no place for her, but Joe's heart felt for the girl, because he knew that her ideal childhood, like the job he adored in this house, would soon end.

'What have you to hide, Miss Teresa? From whom do you need to hide it, miss? Let me guess. You have a secret, perhaps?' He smiled warmly at her, encouraging her to share this trouble. Besides, if there were more trouble brewing in the house, then the sooner Joe knew about it the better. He had a family to support. Her mama understood that others relied upon the household running smoothly, but Mr Johnson did not care and, as for its new master, time would tell, no doubt.

Teresa was standing holding something behind her back. Her eyes were filled with dedication to her task.

Joe thought for a moment that he would have loved to keep her here, as her father would have wished her to stay, but sadly, the handsome young Colonel Matthews would not be coming back from his overseas service. She would make a fine playmate for his girl and his son, Ben. Joe sighed. The lad, he knew, was also aware of how the young child he had played with so freely whilst her mother was busy had turned from an active, fun-filled lass to one whose shape and clothes were changing. Joe put those notions aside.

Ben was his son, the son of a common man, not suitable for one like the young miss, but Joe suspected that Ben had matured beyond his years and looked upon his playmate as something more. One way or the other hearts here would soon be broken or smashed. So what was her mama to do, with no husband to care for her? Joe wiped his face with the back of his sleeve. If only he were fifteen years younger and a lot richer, he thought, he'd take on the young mistress and she could raise a whole brood. He'd like that, very much.

'Yes, it is a secret, in a way. However, you must promise to keep it to yourself, Joseph.' Large blue eyes stared at him, as mysterious and captivating as the sea's depth, trusting and determined. So like her father's, he mused. He had served under Matthews and had admired the man greatly.

'Why are you telling Joe, then?' He sat down on a three-legged stool and faced her.

'Because you have a shovel and we need it,' she said quietly, still glancing over her shoulder to check the yard was clear of anyone from the house.

'Why would we need a shovel?' He folded his arms over his leather waistcoat that protected his ample belly.

'To bury my treasure of course,' she whispered. Slowly, she brought her hand from around the back of her pretty dress and showed him a black and gold coloured tin box, which was secured by a simple key lock. Then, with the fingers of her other hand she pulled up a ribbon from around her neck, which had been tied like a necklace and on which hung a small black key. 'Mama said that treasures needed to be buried deep.'

'And what have you hidden away in there?' He put his hand out for the box, but she quickly tucked the key back in its hiding place still clinging to the tin.

'I haven't. It's a secret, and one which I must keep safe for a long time. Mama said it is my treasure and I must keep it till I'm all grown up and can understand what it means. She said not to look at it now, or else it will bring me bad luck. I am to bury it where no one would ever find it. So I need a spade and you — we must hide it, somewhere safe, so that no one can steal it away from me.' She placed the tin box in Joe's hand.

'You want to bury your treasure?' Joe had to swallow. Whatever was in that tin, he knew would have to be kept safe.

'Did your mama know you are asking me?' Joe saw her cheeks flush, guilt seeped into her expression.

'No, but I thought you'd be able to bury it deeper and safer than me. I trust you not to say a word — like when Ben and I got wet in the rain. You didn't tell Mama about that, did you?'

Joe nearly laughed out loud. He stifled his instinct to guffaw, because it would have been worth more than his position to admit he let her play on the dunes with Ben. Besides, the lad would have had a beating for sure and no one took a stick to his son. His own childhood had been filled with enough of them.

'Will you help me?' she asked.

For a moment he could not speak. He was an old soldier; he had fought the Sultan's army in India. Joe had seen things that no man should, even doubted if he were on the side he should be at times as foreign lands were claimed, yet the naivety of a small child coupled with the kindness of her mama, made his eyes moist. What to do now then? he asked himself. 'Why don't you put it under your bed or in your cabinet? That way you can keep a safe eye upon it. Your mama has not been well. She may change her mind when she has had time to think about it with a clear head.'

'Because, if I did that, Mrs Shellow would find it when she snoops — she does you know, when I am not there, and then she would tell Mr Johnston and I don't want that. Mama said it was for me only when I am older!' she whispered her words, but the determination spilled through every word.

'Miss Teresa, has anyone told you why your mama would give you such a thing at this time?' He placed his hands firmly around the tin in a protective manner.

'Because she wants me to have something precious, she told me so. So now we must find a place to bury it.' Teresa was looking around the small room until her eyes rested on the shovel she sought. She took a step toward it, but Joe stopped her.

'Miss Teresa, you must not get those pretty slippers dirty here or Mrs Shellow will know for sure where you have been. You go and put something more suitable on your feet and I will bring your tin and my spade and we shall find somewhere to keep your treasure safe.' He winked at her as he stood up cradling the precious box to his side nestled in the crook of his arm.

'Thank you, Joe. But I cannot find my boots. I think Mrs Shellow has put them somewhere. She is sneaky. Tell me where you will place it and I will return to my room as I have to change into my travel attire, then she may return my boots to me! We are all going to take a trip to York.' She glanced over her shoulder again.

'Oh, so you do know that you are leaving then.' He picked up the spade with his free hand.

'I am going on a trip.' Her words were repeated as Teresa's young head spun around. She looked as though she had sensed there was something wrong. She stopped watching the yard for a moment and, instead, her eyes searched his face. 'Why do you look so sad, Joe? I am going on a trip with Mama, that is all. We are to see the city and stay as guests of Mr Johnston's sister. She has a school there and whilst we stay I shall be taught. Then I will be back here of course!'

'I shall dig a hole by end of the stable block. Two paces past the stand pipe and a good three feet down.' He placed her tin in a piece of sacking and tied it neatly with a leather strap. 'There it shall be safe and protected. Now you go and have a good journey and don't you worry none. Joe shall keep your treasure safe.' He forced a smile onto his face.

'I will come back, Joe . . . I will,' she answered, as she backed away.

Joe nodded, as his words failed to materialise as he watched the girl hesitantly take in his meaning, then as quickly as she had arrived, she flitted off like a butterfly on a summer's day. Not a thought had she given or a message uttered for his Ben. Joe sighed. She was set to break hearts and the first one he she would succeed in shattering, he feared, would be that of his kind-hearted son.

'Aye, lass, that you will,' he answered quietly to himself, knowing it highly unlikely. He stood waving to her as she ran back toward the house.

Joe set the little box down on his workbench and without hesitation he unwrapped it. He then looked around for a fine file, one he used for delicate jobs and set to picking the lock free. His career before being that of a solider had been one formed in the streets of the notorious Seven Dials in London. He had found the skills he learned there, plying his various trades of survival, extremely useful over the years. Life on this remote coast was very different; here he could breathe fresh air, catch fresh fish and exist without looking over his shoulder all the time. Within seconds he had released the catch on the tin and was inside the precious box.

Joe glanced out of the doorway. The lass had returned to the cosseted environment of the house, leaving her precious gift in his trust. He shook his head. No one would have ever have trusted 'Joseph Lamb' like that child did. He shook his head, lifted the lid and felt unworthy. The girl would never return, her precious treasure would be forgotten and the naive child would be disciplined until she lost any trait of her natural naivety. Soon the cosseted love would be replaced by resentment as she was separated from her mama and forced to do the bidding of some teacher in a school, whose main aim would be to make the child grow into a woman — an obedient and subservient one. Her world would be run by the values of Mr Johnston, and her poor ma would watch in silence, because a sensitive child would be no good in the marriage market. She would need to be able to raise her own brood in not that many more years. He knew . . . she didn't, but time would show her, and in time, all she now valued as treasure and precious would be forgotten, like Joe and this tin box. He removed the contents, locked the tin and collected his spade. He'd not gone back on his word. Joe would bury the tin. Its contents he placed deep in his pocket — safe . . . for later.

Ben watched his pa from the corner of the scullery. He had seen Teresa tiptoe over to the work room and felt that strange sense of excitement rise within him. Only it had quickly abated as he realised she was not looking for him. It seemed that she came out of the house less and less. When she did she was dressed in ridiculous clothes for doing anything like they used to. An awkward silence had ensued the last time he saw her by the church. She could hardly look in his direction.

Before he made his presence known he saw his pa take out of the tin her precious secret. Why? He felt a cold fear creep up his body from the bottom of his stomach. His pa was an honourable man, so why would he do such a thing. He stayed stock still and watched as his father took the empty tin and his spade and fulfilled his promise. He buried the tin deep. Ben swallowed as he leaned against the stable and watched from the shadows. His friend was leaving, apparently, and his pa hid secrets. Soon he too would go. He had already decided that he would join the army and fight for his country as his pa before him had done.

* * *

The next morning the villagers lined the road from Marsh Farm as the carriage was prepared and luggage was loaded onto a wagon which went ahead of them. Ben leaned against the wall of the house, out of sight until he saw Teresa step out of the house in her plum coloured velvet travel coat with matching bonnet. She looked so fine, he thought and, for the first time within her presence, he felt grubby and tattered as he stepped forward.

'Teresa!' he said, pointedly, desperate to catch her attention before Shellow or her ma saw him.

Teresa looked around, saw him and took a few steps to within a few feet of him. 'What is it, Ben?' she asked.

'I made you something — something to remember the place by,' he smiled, hoping she would. Those deep blue pools of eyes looked at him curiously. 'Here,' he said casually, and tossed it to her.

She caught the small object in her lace hand. It was a hair slide, made from whale bone and carved; scrimshaw was his hobby, encouraged by his pa. It had taken him hours to try to make the teeth even and the design of sea horses and flowers had been the best work he had ever done. He smiled broadly at her as she rolled it over in her hand.

'It is fine, Ben. Look, mama will not approve of me having this now. You keep it safe till I return. Then I shall wear it when we walk upon the beach again.' She placed it in his hand.

He felt the touch of her fine laced glove and the coarseness of his gift made him swallow. She had fine things of a lady. He coloured deeply, shrugged and was about to walk off whilst he could still nurture some dignity, when she was summoned.

'Teresa, come. What do you think you are doing?' Mrs Shellow ushered her into the carriage to join her mother.

Ben watched from the building.

When the coach moved forward he ran to the gate and was there as she passed by. Teresa raised that same gloved hand in a final wave, but her mama's black gloved hand pulled down the coach window's blind before he could return the gesture.

Ben swallowed again as his guts churned, his eyes watered and he felt his heart would die. His hand wrapped around the comb and he placed it deep in his pocket. He stood tall as Joe walked over to him. Rejection was hard to face, when there was no way he could overcome it.

'She's gone, lad.' He placed a hand on Ben's shoulder.

'She'll return, I know it.' Ben stared ahead at the back of the coach.

'No, lad, she won't. You set your stall too high. She isn't for the likes of us.' Joe sucked on his long clay pipe.

'You're wrong. If I am not good enough now, then I shall set out to be so. In five years I will have made my fortune!' Ben said.

'Not for her, lad,' Joe said softly.

Ben pulled away. 'You'll see, so shall she.' He sniffed and turned away, first walking and then running toward the dunes.

# 1

## Eight Years Later

Teresa walked into the morning room. Her mama was bent over her needle-point. Her hand was unsteady; it never used to be so. In the months since she had returned to her, it was apparent that her health had suffered in their years apart. If only things could have been different. 'Mama, I was wondering . . . '

'What are you wondering this time, Teresa? Is it a walk, or a visit to the Minster that you desire?' Her mother sighed.

'Well, yes, but not a walk. I wondered about a trip.' Teresa paused but her mother did not look up. She hated the constant need of a chaperone; why could she not walk free? Or run if that was what she felt like doing. There had once been a time when she had run wild with a young boy from the village. He had been the odd-job man's son, older than her and somewhat awkward she remembered but a fitter companion she had never known or had since. Then, she also remembered that these adventures had happened when her mama was abed still or visiting elsewhere.

'Ah . . . Cecilia has told her of her visit. You have heard about the waters at Harrogate? They do not work, I have been. They taste awful and do nothing for the spirits at all.' She continued to sew.

'No, I would not inflict that upon you, or myself, although a visit to such a place might do you the power of good. However, I think that the sea air's refreshing properties on your face would bring fresh colour to your cheeks.' Teresa continued, hedging nearer her true request.

'And a chill to my bones no doubt!' She chuckled. 'I had enough of the 'benefits' of the sea air when I married your father, child.' She shuddered as if dismissing the memory.

Teresa felt uneasy, sensing her next request would be far from well received, but also the time to ask may well be now or never.

'Why don't we go to see Uncle in Alunby? It is years since we were at Marsh Hall Farm. I have such fond memories of the place and . . . ' Her mother's fingers stopped mid air as if suspended in time, ' . . . Alunby should look grand at this time of the year. The bullrushes will be at full height on the marshland and . . . '

Her mother's impassive face lifted up from her work, but her grey blue eyes had a hard, defiant edge to them as they met Teresa's hopeful ones.

'Teresa, I have told you many times, my dear. We cannot return to Alunby, not even for a short visit, not ever.' She placed her needlepoint down into her tapestry bag that was tucked in by her feet.

Teresa looked at her mother squarely. The grey hair pulled back and up onto her head, neatly pinned had no fleck of its natural dark brown. She had poise, though, as her prim figure was sitting upright upon the chair by the window of their home, the chin tilted slightly upwards to reinforce her words. This terrace house was in a fashionable area of York and, no doubt, was the envy of many, but since Teresa had returned the previous spring from her enforced education at The Abbey School she had grown to hate it, not quite as much as the school, but almost. The abbey had been no more than a village church, and her home had been the shared room in the loft space of the nearby school house.

'Surely we may visit, Uncle. I am certain he would like to see us again. Can you not ask your husband, Mama?' Teresa was pushing the point, ignoring the edge to her mama's voice. She realised that this may not be wise, but her spirit and longing was too strong to deny a voice.

'That is quite enough harrowing for one day! Your father will not wish you to go away again so soon, when you are only recently returned to us. He cannot take me back to the home where I once lived, it would not be proper! Your father wishes you to meet people here.' She stood up. Her eyes lacked the sparkle they had had once, even if her voice was still spirited. 'You are a young woman with prospects and an education, you need to be here to meet people and make yourself known in society.

'He is not my father, Mama. He never will be! You referred to my true father and my original home, how can you then refer to Mr Johnston as my father now?' Teresa had not moved. She did not speak in arrogance, but she spoke the truth. Mr Johnston may have taken her father's place in her mother's bed, but she would never accept him as anything other than the man who separated her from the last members of her true family — her mother and her uncle.

Teresa saw the hurt in her mother's eyes and regretted her hasty words. She did not want to cause her any more pain, but there was no one else she could share her frustration with, or displace her anger upon.

'He has paid for all of this. The house you take shelter in, the bed you sleep in, the clothes your wear upon your back and the food you eat. Not to mention your education. He saved us from being turned out into a fisherman's cottage and a life of shame and poverty. Can you not show him some respect now? Has he not done enough for you as any father should? He could not have done more, child!' She faced her daughter.

Teresa did not want to remember the 'education' she had been privileged to sharing with the other poor girls. It had been more like free labour, long hours making lace, and mending, making, baking and cleaning, occasionally learning words, numbers and of course the verses from the Bible — especially anything to do with toiling, being wretched or humble. The beatings had not been severe, but frequent enough. The skill of the perpetrator made them sting without marking. Then in the last two years she had been moved into a proper bedroom in the old house adjacent to the school with another girl. Her final grooming had begun. She was then taught how to run the house, what to wear when, how to address people and to know a woman's place. 'How much have you paid, Mama, over these long years for his generosity, whilst we have been apart? What has been the true cost of your life here?' She took a step towards her mama and held out her hand. The woman looked at it, but did not take it within her own. She looked as if she was considering slapping it away.

'You are ungrateful for all I have given you! You consider only your own wants and do not give one notion for what has been provided for you,' her mother replied and bit her bottom lip. 'Go to your room. You have vexed me. I need to calm myself before dinner. I will not have Mr Johnston upset by your lack of respect and gratitude.' She turned away and stared out of the long panelled window into the street beyond, apparently watching the vendors plying their various trades. Beyond the solitude of the house, the bustle outside had a perpetual momentum.

'Mama, I would have been happy to have lived in a simple fisherman's cottage with you. It would not have been so bad, Mama, not as long as we were together. He sent me away from you. We only saw each other at Easter, in the summer and then for a week at Christmas! I missed you so much . . . ' Teresa stepped back as her mother swung around, her eyes flashing with anger as she stared back at her.

'It would not have been so bad, would it? With nowhere to wash in private which is clean and nothing new to wear, but the same clothes day in day out getting shabbier as each year passes. The locals laughing at us, as the fallen wenches from the hall! Or worse, the likes of Joseph Lamb's pitying eyes upon me, as he wished he could support me and my child along with his own brat, no doubt — very convenient.' Her eyes, like her words, were cold and cruel. 'Could you imagine that — your mama and the hired help? Just because of some misplaced loyalty to my first husband, who had no more sense than to run off to war leaving me with a child and never bothering to return to either of us. Oh what a hero he turned out to be and Joe forever paying tribute to such a great man as he.'

'He died a hero,' Teresa said defensively, remembering the shabby man who had filled her head as a child with stories of the colonel's bravery, loyalty and devotion to the safety of his men.

'He died! He left me and deserted you. That is the kind of man he was.'

She paused only whilst she sniffed. 'Meanwhile 'your uncle' would take over our home, gloating. He had always said he should have been the eldest brother. I turned him down you see, but he was always there, always waiting for my spirit to bend to his will so that he could finally have what he had always longed for . . . ' she turned her head away, 'but I would never give him that satisfaction of knowing he had won. Not even for you, my dear ungrateful child.'

'What do you mean?' Teresa asked, dreading the answer. Her uncle had always been an intimidating figure, but he was her father's brother and that meant family. Surely, she reasoned, he had not threatened her mother in some way. He was her only brother-in-law. She gasped and looked aghast as the meaning of the threat sank in.

'So the child has grown up a little and for once can see what was in front of her eyes, yet she could not see it because of her naivety. Well consider what your mama has sheltered her from. See, Teresa, you and your thoughtless words have angered me again. You always were a spirited child. I had hoped that the school would have strengthened your flesh, but humbled your soul, but it appears it strengthened your body and made your mind even more determined than it was as a selfish child.' She closed up her needlepoint bag and left it upon the window seat. 'And now I can see I have obviously said too much of the truth, something you have never been able to deal with effectively and no doubt you will sulk.' There was an icy chill to her words, which Teresa found unnerving. This was not the mother she remembered as a child, nor the one she had visited in the few holidays which had been allowed. This woman was a stranger to her.

'You knew what the school was going to be like, yet you let him take me there?' Teresa felt unsteady on her feet as she spoke. She had always presumed that her mother had been made to part with her. Their holidays had been so happy that she had not wanted to part miserably so had not pleaded with her to stay, but hoped that somehow her mother would keep her with her and not send her back. Always, Mr Johnston was around to see that they were well and to restrict the opportunity for Teresa to talk too openly with her mama, or so she had thought. Two shocks within a few minutes had rocked her understanding of her mother and her uncle. 'I never knew uncle threatened you, or had made any such ugly suggestions to you. I didn't realise he could have been so evil as to prey upon a widow, particularly his own brother's.' She shook her head as if trying to dismiss the images filling her mind; her playing as a child with this man, an ogre, totally unaware of what was happening in the adult realm around her. 'I thought . . . I just wanted to be with you again. I did not think you received my letters from the school, that was when I was able to write them.

I thought Mr Johnston must have stopped them from reaching you, but you knew all along how miserable I was without you there . . . ' Teresa swallowed.

'You had to grow up, Teresa. This world is a harsh place. You were a child and innocent, but I was all alone, a woman in a world made for men. I chose a good one over a bad one, and trusted that you would be given a way of cracking out of your own invisible world, fuelled by your father's lackey from the wars, to be given an education and a chance to find a decent match. But that spirit of yours is as stubborn as your father's before you — yes, I mean your blood one, and I can tell you now it will never do! You must hide it from the world. Turn it into determination to raise your own family, whatever the cost to you, and be a good wife. There is no other way for us and you have to learn to bow to it.'

'What of happiness? Does it count for nothing in this world you have chosen for me?' Teresa asked.

'Have you not learnt anything of this world, girl? Happiness is a hidden treasure. If you can find it in a passing moment then savour it whilst it lasts, but don't expect it to linger, or your heart will break. It visits on occasion but never stays for long.' Her mother held out her hand and this time it was Teresa who held it, loosely though.

Her mama was satisfied that all was well between them, but what she had said had hardened Teresa more than the years at the school. It had shown her that the image she had of her mama was false, seen through the eyes of the child that she had once been. Somewhere in the back of her memory, though, her words had rekindled an image of her old friend Joe. How could she have forgotten about him; he was always so kind to her? Also, 'the brat' her mother referred to, the boy, Bob . . . Bert . . . Ben! He had been so easy to be with. She smiled but there was something else niggling at her

33

mind, also. It was to do with something to hide . . . '

'Well we are far away from all of that now. No more school for you and no more Alunby ever for either of us,' her mother said reassuringly . . . at least for her.

Teresa's memory recalled a tin box, a promise and her own special treasure. She smiled. Would it still be there? Would Joe be?

Her mother responded, instantly, misreading the look of hope, which had spread across Teresa's face. 'Now go and change for dinner and make no more of this nonsense, you hear me?' Her mother patted her gently on her shoulder. 'Mr Johnston will want us both to be present at the table as he has something he wishes to talk to you about. Now run along and remember to nurture an attitude which is becoming and selfless.'

'Yes, Mama,' Teresa replied, and had to stop herself from skipping out of the room as the child would have done to appease a difficult parent. She had to find a way of returning to Alunby, to Marsh Hall and find her old friend Joe. Would he still be there? He must be, she reasoned, he had a spade and he would remember where the treasure was buried. Her destiny, she decided, was there, buried and forgotten, but it was hers to rediscover.

# 2

Benjamin rode towards the coast from the moor road. It had been an hour since he had passed the ancient monument of Whitby Abbey on his right, with its stark outline silhouetted against the grey sky as it stood boldly upon the headland. He flicked his reins and drove his horse on with a feeling of exhilaration pumping through his veins as he neared the place he had known as home for the first fourteen years of his life. He had missed his father and the endless tales of his time in India, and then later in the first two years of the Peninsular war in Spain. It was here that he was sent home, injured, but fortunately not beyond repair. He smiled inwardly at the wealth of warm memories that flooded his tired brain. Although home should have been to the poverty of the Dials in London, he instead was offered a place to recuperate, and build a new life on the estate his officer had owned. It had been Ben's home and the place he longed to return to as a man in his own right. His belly ached with hunger, but his heart was filled with the desire to see his humble home again. He held such memories of it. The fair haired beauty who had left it, he hoped had returned. He prayed he was not too late, but knew in his heart, he was expecting a lot to find her there waiting.

Benjamin's body was tired of the constant travelling. From London he had taken the coach to Selby and from there he had continued on horseback. He had ridden persistently only stopping at one of the inns when he had to, to rest the horse and feed himself. He followed the track that led down through the gill down toward the sandy bay of Seaham. Tempting as it was to follow the familiar path to the inn at the bottom, where Annie Barton's ale would welcome him, he ignored the impulse to visit the old inn by the beach. He knew the curious faces that turned towards the strangers as he entered the outskirts of the old village; but none recognised him. He was a man full grown now, not a hapless lad from the old marsh village along the coast. 'Swampy' they had cruelly jibed at him as a youngster, when he had walked along the beach to this end of the bay on his own. He did not forget such things. Small minds, he thought to himself. He had travelled the world whilst they had stayed still. These folk were still carrying out the same chores now as then: mending nets, stacking lobster pots and gutting fish. No doubt the same superstitions and fears haunted them, now as then.

From the shore at Seaham, he took to the sands as the tide was well out. Here he let the horse have its head as he rode the length of the bay past Masham, Ebton and Fissleham to his home village of Alunby, which nestled at the start of the old marshland. He turned off the beach at this point and made his tired horse pick up its pace again as it found the track to the village, he saw the old row of cottages ahead of him. He was shocked to see newer buildings behind them. New buildings lined the road, all of the new streets led down to the dunes. The place had changed not quite beyond recognition but drastically. It was not the village he knew anymore. He could not see the old buildings of Marsh Hall Farm. Instead of the higgledy-piggledy collection of rambling outhouses around the main hall building there was a wall, gates that overshadowed the remnants of what had once been a tiny, but an open, hamlet.

He dismounted by the first cottage, secured the reins to an iron loop which was fixed to its wall and walked along to the cottage he recognised as his old home. There was no one inside. Opening the door he peered inside. His father's old rocking chair was not there. It was not the only piece of familiar furniture to be missing. Neither was his old coat or the boots by the side of the door. Even the old kettle, which always rested on the hearth, was different. It had totally changed. He ran along the line of single story buildings, carrying his kit bag, searching, frantically looking for his father. He had dreamed of this moment, but his dream had not been like this, though. In those moments of created bliss Benjamin had found his father sitting on his stool outside the work room by the old stables at the back of the hall, the man's face etched on his mind as he had visualised the look of sheer joy as the father greeted his son once more. He spun around on the spot, leaning against the wall of the old cottage, staring up and down this strange street as he realised — it had all changed. There was no old work room to be seen anymore and his father was definitely not there. Panic was replacing excitement as he looked at the emptiness, which echoed the black chasm of disappointment within his own heart.

When he had left there had only been this one row of old cottages known simply as Marsh Street. The village had grown and now there were others lined with houses: Sand Street, Field Street, Warren Lane and a small chapel at the end of Widgeon Lane. The old church of St Cuthbert stood at the end of the small village.

He had been away for nearly six years. Not by choice, but because his duty had called him away to a foreign land to serve his King and country. He looked around for anyone he recognised. The old cottages looked as if they would be dwarfed by this new township. Once, many years since, this had been a natural harbour town, quite wealthy and known for its salt works. Those days were long gone before his life had began.

He stood back, leaned against some old crab pots stacked by the end cottage and watched, trying to decide what to do and where he should go.

There were few people around. Surely someone would be here from his old life; he peered up the streets for anyone whom he recognised. The small row of dwellings behind him looked even more run down than he had remembered, as they were now side by side with newer larger ones.

Benjamin was tired, dusty, dirty and hungry and desperately wanting to see his father. He had sent word home several times, but his father could neither read nor write more than his name, so he had no knowledge of what had been happening here having never received word back. The church seemed to be the best place to go to enquire as to where his father may be. He swallowed; surely he was not too late. 'Pray to God he lives and is in sound mind,' he thought. He could go and ask at the hall, but thought that perhaps, if there was bad news, it would be better to go to someone who would know him. That is, if Reverend Sigston was still ministering there. Perhaps even he has changed, he wondered.

'Oi, there!' shouted a rough voice from the house at the end of Widgeon Lane nearest him.

He turned his head to find the owner of it. Some tone of familiarity gave him hope. It was one of the old biddies who he had grown up around. 'Yes!' he exclaimed aloud as he recognised the stout figure of old Ida.

'It's me, Ida, young Ben, isn't it.'

He quickened his step as he almost ran to her dropping his bag and sweeping her up in his arms, swinging her around so that she dropped her wicker basket onto the ground.

'Put me down, you young whipper-snapper.' She wriggled as he placed her worn boots back on the sandy earth. Her hand clamped her grubby cloth cap to her greying hair. 'Lad, how you have grown! Thee would have all the lasses after you now, wouldn't thee. You are a sight for sore and very tired eyes! Ee, lad, we thought you might have been killed like the colonel was. Ee, I can't get over you turning up like this, man, how we grieved for thee. So long you've been gone and not a word of thee.' She held his arms and looked at him as if taking in the fact he was there in front of her, and yet she could not believe it. 'You is a man full grown, whiskers and all.'

'I sent letters back here, care of Marsh Hall Farm. I was . . . we were held prisoners for some time. It has not been easy finding my way back here, Ida, but I cannot wait to see Pa and tell him I am here to take care of him again. Where is he?' He pointed down the row. 'The cottage has changed so much there is no trace of his things. Did they move him into one of these new places? It does not look like my home anymore. What happened here? Everything has changed so much.'

'He was so affeared that you had gone the way of the colonel. It nearly tore his heart apart with grief for thee. Shame that man had not survived for he would have made a good master of the hall, unlike 'his self!' She glared in the direction of the Marsh Hall. 'You sent your letters there? The evil wretch! I bet he read 'em and used them for kindling. He is as tight as a rabbit's snare.' She glowered at the hall. 'Come, lad. Best not stay out here where 'hisself' might see us.'

It was then he studied the added buildings to the hall: the higher wall, which went right the way around the grounds and the large iron gates, dominating the front façade. The stable block and work room where his father had done most of his chores when Ben was a child had been rebuilt. Gone was the old low lying single storey building and in its place was a fine brick built construction with a bell tower at its centre. The old stables had been removed by this larger longer extension, which now had all the outbuildings housed under one roof and edged a quadrangle, leaving a sort of courtyard inside the gates.

'Where's my Pa, Ida?' he asked,

noticing that instantly the smile on Ida's weatherworn face vanished. The lines creased as she almost grimaced at the question.

'Oh, lad, he's not lived here for nigh on a year.' She shook her head again bobbing her bonnet to and fro. ''Tis no good, you had better calm tha self. Come inside, come on . . . ' she tugged at his sleeve, but his eyes were transfixed as he stared at the new buildings which had taken over his memories of his home, as if trying to stamp them out.

Ben was shocked by this news and feared that his father was already dead. If he had returned too late to save him, he would never be able to forgive himself. What use was a son when a man was in need, if he died feeling deserted and alone or had lost hope that he would find a way home? 'Is he . . . '

'Lad, you best come with me inside, out of harm's way. There's been a lot of changes around these parts. Come in and rest those tired legs of yours and I will set you straight on what's been happening, but lad, you must keep a cool head, if you is to do your father any good at all.'

'He lives then?' Ben blurted out.

'Aye, lad, he lives. But his is not a happy lot and he will need you. Come on, Ben, stay with the living and stop day-dreaming,' she said, and tugged his arm firmly this time.

With these ominous words dashing around his mind he followed the woman as she limped back into her new home. Ben stooped down to pick up her discarded basket and carried it inside for her. He was bracing himself for some unfathomable truth, which although he did not know how, had some connection with those gates, the wall and the destruction of Ben's old space, his father's precious workshop.

'Ida, tell me where he is and while there is still some daylight I will go to him.' He placed the basket down at the side of the hearth where the remnants of a flame dwindled amongst the coals.

'Not that simple, Benjamin. He lives and as far as we know he is still sound in body, but he needs thee to rescue him from where he is kept. Sit down and have some bread and brandy — you'll need it and don't ask where Ida gets it from, but it's good liquor, lad, and kept well hid.'

'Kept?' Benjamin repeated.

'Aye, lad, kept away from prying eyes.' She winked.

'Not the brandy, you said Pa was kept.' He watched the expression on her face as she stared unblinkingly back at him.

'That's right and I did not mean the brandy. I meant your pa. They have him in the infirmary, he is locked in there and the likes of Ida could not have him released. It will take an heducated man like yourself to do that.'

Ben knelt down on one knee by her chair. 'Where is he? Tell me where they have him and I will rip the place apart with my bare hands if I need to get him out!'

'No, lad, that you will not, or I will not tell thee anything. Be calm. Sit and Ida will explain further.'

# 3

Teresa had ignored her mother's instruction and instead she had gone for an amble down the busy street toward the coaching inn. She knew that it was not a place she should venture alone. In fact, walking alone in the street was far from what her mama would consider respectable. What she thought her school days had been like Teresa had often wondered, for there she had been no better than a pair of hands free to chore, and legs that would take her on many an errand for her lazy mistress. Yet, they had forced the 'rough lass' as she was referred to into the trappings of a young lady for the purpose of returning her to her home. Now, she was supposed to sit, read, do needless sewing tasks and await a suitor to be found for her; enticed, entrapped and matched as her mother and the 'perfect' Mr Johnston dictated.

She looked up toward the sunlight that filtered through the pale blue sky. Perhaps her days of running errands had more to offer her than this. Teresa had been allowed outside on these tasks and had enjoyed her burst of freedom. Remembering Joe, the hired hand who seemed to be a mine of information about anything to do with surviving outdoors, she smiled. The thought of seeing his grizzled face again filled her with happiness. Surely his world would not have changed, nor Joe. His existence stayed constant for years. Teresa could picture him still sitting upon his stool at his workbench, the spade on the nail behind him on the wall. One thing would have changed, she realised, was that his older face would have more lines and he may not move as easily as he had before. But she knew in her heart he would still be there waiting for her to retrieve her precious treasure. His sort were reliable, they were dependable and loyal. His life would have remained untouched by the pressures she had had to endure, of this she was quite certain. She wondered if her uncle had taken himself a wife. Perhaps he was over his infatuation with her mother and had forgiven her rejection of him. She was certain her mother's cool demeanour could have upset him, so perhaps her viewpoint had been skewed by the loss of her husband. He may have been offering her a way of staying within the home her husband had left. After all, she had had no property of her own. Teresa could not imagine her uncle turning them out into a cottage, it would show him to be a rogue and no one would respect him. No, her mother was deluding herself to justify her acceptance of Johnston.

Teresa stopped at a milliners, supposedly admiring their display. She ignored the woman inside, who desperate to have her make purchases at her establishment, gestured she should go inside. Teresa did not; instead she ventured to a draper and then called in at a friend's house to see her latest joy, a baby. Listening to the details of the birth, which, to Teresa, was the most persuasive argument she had ever heard as to why a young woman should avoid the condition of matrimony, her thoughts returned to her carefree days of Alunby. All the while, Teresa nodded to her friend, whilst thinking of how she, as a single woman, could enquire as to purchasing a coach ticket which would take her first to the market town of Gorebeck, from where she could get a local coach to Ebton, which was the nearest reachable town within walking distance of Alunby, although not so if she was travelling with her trunk. She realised if she was to do this bold and damning act, she could be foiled at any of the points along the route. It would be so easy to trace her. Not only that, but her rash act would ruin her reputation for all to see. No, it was too cavalier an act to do so so openly; she would or could be recognised along the way.

As she walked back towards her

home, or Mr Johnston's as she thought of it, refusing to consider it as her own, avoiding the bustle of people along the street and trying not to become spattered by the many users of the muddied road, she knew there had to be another way. Perhaps, she wondered, if she managed to take a coach to Whitby, she could get a fisherman to take her along the coast and drop her on Alunby sands. It was once a natural harbour point; therefore, landing a coble there should not be a problem. Teresa mulled the thought over, still uneasy about this option. Yes, that was it! Her head shot up and she smiled, but as the Minster stood boldly before her, the vast gothic style cathedral, instantly, her heart sank again because she realised that, that was no good either. She would still be traced from the coach and then how could she be sure to find a trustworthy man with a boat willing to take her safely to such a place without questioning her? If he was willing to do that, he could easily whisk her off to France or somewhere where she could never be traced — to be used or abused. She had heard of such wickedness from her friend, Mabel, who always had some salacious piece of tittle-tattle to spread that she had read about somewhere. Certainly she was not party to the same imprints her mama had within the house. The last visit to see her had been spent with Mabel trying to whisper a fanciful tale to her about a maid, a book and a monk, although he, the monk in question, had not seemed to be of an overly pious nature. She grinned to herself as a rider came rather close and she had to step back into an alleyway to save herself from being knocked aside by the animal.

Cursing him under her breath, she shook her skirt, violently flicking the hem as if that would remove the spatter of mud the horse's hooves had flicked up at her. Then she realised, it was the obvious answer. She would have to ride there. It could not be that hard a destination to find. The road to Gorebeck was clearly marked on the old Roman way; straight as a die. From there, she would venture east to the coast and, she suspected, north again. If she rode early and kept going she might be able to make just the one stop at Gorebeck. Yes, that was it. She had her plan, now she had to be careful as to how she slipped away. Timing and planning would be the making or breaking of it. She was sure Mr Johnston was going to Harrogate for a couple of days. Her mama was always lost as to make a decision without him, so if she went then, by the time he heard about her disappearance then she would be back home in Alunby. She would present herself to her uncle as if a message that she was coming had gone astray, and then have him send word that she was safe, and then seek her box, her treasure and tell Joe all about life at the horrid school. She would make her own mind up about her uncle. She was certain that her mama's grief at losing her pa had affected her deeply and twisted her vision of what was actually happening. Her uncle may have been offering her a home in his house and she, being sensitive and under the influence of Johnston, had been persuaded his intentions were ignoble. Teresa, developed this theory so much that her musings became an acceptable and realistic truth, so with her mind set on her new plan she took heart that she would have her treasure, whatever it was, her mama had also forgotten about it. But more than this childish whim, she had a vision — Teresa would reunite her family in the home she believed that they should never have left.

Excited by the prospect of her quest she greeted her mama with unusual enthusiasm on entering the morning room, and then skipped up the stairs to her room to change out of her attire and plan her next move. She would need a change of clothes, some essential items and some coin. Even if she had to return with the shame hanging over her head at least, Teresa thought, she would have done something exciting and lived through an adventure. Besides, she reasoned, her treasure might make her independent. Her mama had told her to keep it safe, for it held a secret value, that one day she would understand.

If only she could ask her mama now what it was, then it would save her the trip and the trouble of going. But, did she dare mention it to her? If she did recall it and then she asked her daughter to return it, then that would leave her in a very awkward position. It puzzled her, though, why her mama had never asked about it now that she was grown and had returned home. Surely something of value would help them both in their situation. Although, Teresa knew only too well that her mama did not think of herself as being trapped in any way. So instead, Teresa continued her usual daily routine of accompanying her mama with needle-point, or later on in the day, a visit to some incessantly boring and dull friend, as any good daughter would. This time though, she was completely distracted by her own thoughts and desires.

It was only when she tried to retire early to bed that she realised her mama, had not been unaware of her detached mood.

'Teresa, sit with me a while, dear.' She patted the seat next to her.

'Yes, Mama, if you wish me to.' She seated herself on the sofa with her mama next to the warmth of the fire. Mr Johnston was drinking his port in his office, seeing to his affairs as he often chose to do for an hour in the evening.

'Tell me, Teresa, does something trouble you — you seemed distracted throughout dinner?' Her mama looked at her curiously.

'I was just thinking about how much has changed since I was away. I suppose

I need time to adjust to being home again. I am sorry if I appeared rude earlier in any way. I do appreciate all that you have intended to be done for me, which was for my own good. I think I am just tired, Mama.' She edged forward.

Her mama placed her hand upon her daughter's. Teresa edged no further. 'What do you think of Mr Brigton, Teresa?'

'Who?' Teresa was racking the depths of her memory trying to remember where she had heard the man's name before.

'Mr Brigton, the gentleman Mr Johnston was talking of at dinner.' Her mama slipped Teresa's hand onto her own. 'You really need to be more attentive to what Mr Johnston says, Teresa. He is your papa now and he has your best interests at heart. Mr Brigton is twenty-seven, the nephew of the Brigton's of Hewerton, a very desirable person for a young lady such as you, Teresa. With his fortune and the dowry that Mr Johnston is prepared to settle upon you, this is a very exciting opportunity that we have here. They have a number of manufactories throughout the county, my dear. He is a young man who stands to inherit a fortune when his uncle dies . . . ' Her mama tilted her head to one side and smiled at her daughter. 'He is a fine looking young man and is coming here this weekend for dinner. His uncle will not give him his inheritance unless he sees him happily wed before he dies. The young man has enjoyed the freedom of bachelorhood and now realises he needs to be more 'settled'. We have arranged this because he has made it known to Mr Johnston that he wants a wife and he has seen you, my dear, and found you to appeal to his preferences in appearance at least. There will be many men who will be lining their daughters up for the dance at the assembly rooms at the end of next month, but Mr Johnston has acted swiftly on your behalf. He has agreed to fund your future, in the interest of the good of the family, Teresa. He has looked beyond the fact that you are not his own blood and will settle his estate upon your first born son instead.' She leaned back and smiled warmly. Teresa thought her mama looked happier than she had seen her for months, certainly since she had returned home. 'He is prepared to come here and meet you, my dear Teresa. You shall be the first he shall consider seriously as his future wife! I can hardly believe how fortune is shining upon you so soon. My little cherub will be better set in life than ever her mama had the fortune to be. Both Mr Johnston and I hope that he will look no further! You must be your most flattering, appealing and attentive to him. Do not day dream when he speaks and acknowledge his every gesture to you. This is your hour to shine, Teresa. It is not just for yourself but for my good name also and, of course, a way of repaying Mr Johnston for his years of giving to you. If he is taken with you there will be no need for you to come out at all this season other than on the arm of your fiancé to announce the forthcoming wedding. You will have beaten the other girls without them even having a look at what they have missed. I have sent for the dressmaker and you are to have the best dresses Mr Johnston can afford, to make sure that your appearance makes such an impression he will desire no one else!' She let out a long breath as she recovered her composure because her words had run away with her. 'Are you not thrilled at the news?'

Teresa had been smiling at her mother's enthusiasm, swept along by her words. 'Of course, Mama, but surely he will want to meet as many young women as he can. It is his happiness he will want to ensure, surely? Besides, how will it be possible to have attire made by this weekend?'

'It will be perfectly possible, there is time, and money can solve most of the problems in this world, which is why you must make every effort to impress this man. He is educated and has ambition. I understand he wishes to make enough to be able to buy property in London. He is already a member of an impressive gentlemen's club and is about to buy a race horse. They even say he is very sporting and has skill with fencing. Mr Johnston is using all his contacts to try to gain him an invitation to the best clubs in York and Harrogate.' Her eyes were sparkling. She was filled with such hope for Teresa's future, the one that she and Mr Johnston had designed for her, that to say no or raise a question objecting to it would shatter her happiness. So Teresa swallowed and looked pleased, wondering what on earth would happen if she left, this man came for dinner and she was missing. The disappointment would certainly make her mama ill, but the humiliation of the public scandal this man could make of it would seriously damage her. There would be no going back on it. It appeared that her adventure would have to wait until this man had been here, assessed and valued her, and then left. How could she deter him, whilst looking as though she was seriously interested in trapping him? This challenge was going to have to be met with skill and conviction. Politely Teresa excused herself and retired to bed.

★　★　★

'Ida, for God's sake explain yourself. Who has him 'kept' somewhere? You are making no sense at all, but you are tearing my heart apart!' Benjamin stopped, surprised by his own emotional outburst. He was usually so composed, but he was tired and beyond caring about anything other than seeing his father again. Although, not meaning to become threatening in any way to an old woman, at that moment his frustration was such that he felt as if he was capable of shaking the truth from her, at least in his mind he could have.

'I'm sorry, lad. It's just so sad. It's not easy for old Ida to think how to explain this. He seemed so calm and collected then he just went . . . so strange; started acting a bit scary, like he was troubled. His temper grew with it and all. When he no longer was needed at the house, he lost his place at the workshop; he just could not seem to fathom it. It was just as if he thought the world was against him. Then he wouldn't talk to folk, it was as though he did not trust us anymore. He wouldn't listen to us. Who could help him then? No one knew why he was like it. We all thought you must have been killed, but no one had heard for sure. So if he was grieving he was doing it strangely and for no good reason. I mean, you hadn't been and here you are to prove it. He seemed to vent all his anger towards 'hisself' at the hall, but of course there was no reason why the master should listen to his ex-odd-job man. So he never got his time, far as we knew. Perhaps it was cos he was a foreigner to these parts — you know, from London. Perhaps he suddenly lost his mind cos he needed to go home and couldn't.'

'Here was his home, Ida. After all these years don't tell me you people still thought of him as an outsider or a 'foreigner'?' Ben shook his head as Ida looked a little embarrassed and shrugged as they obviously still did think that way.

Ida raised both hands, palms upwards as if to say, it was the truth. Her tongue seemed unable to put into clear words what she was trying to utter, to the point that she could not speak the plain truth to him. Ben swallowed. 'You mean he was angry at something, but no one knew what it was?'

'Lad, he went wild like a fish caught on a hook. He wriggled and would lash out at the slightest thing. He was dangerous, and he burned with a desire, but would not tell us, not even Ezekial at the chapel, what was upsetting him. He even upset the

Reverend by throwing a Bible across the church at him.'

Benjamin spoke up instantly, 'Are you sure?'

'Well he certainly dropped one at his feet as he quoted from it.' Ida shrugged as if it was an understandable exaggeration. Then she picked up her story, finding her words with enthusiasm now she had begun the tale. 'Joe wanted to cause trouble. He was openly rude to 'hisself' from Marsh Hall, shouting at him as he came out of the gates in his fine carriage.

'What did he say? What did he shout at him?'

'Oh, how can I remember that, Ben? It was something about bad blood. Told you he had not got over losing his position there. He had bad blood over that for sure. But why should 'hisself' mind or care? He tossed his own fine sister-in-law and that lovely lass out without giving thought to it at all.'

Benjamin remembered the young girl, Teresa, well, and her endless energy and love of all things she shouldn't have. Like climbing the old tree, running after him up and down the dunes and taking a line with him when the tide was out to the end of the rocks; always daring themselves to stay there until they caught a fish and then the panic and cold fear as he had to swim her back to the shore when the tide had cut them off without him realising what had been happening. Teresa was like that, she was absorbing even as a child, he was mesmerised by her — still was. He had got such a deserved thrashing from his pa for that one. She caught a chill, but her mother was none the wiser as to how she had come by it. The girl had been sent away and his life was a lot duller as a consequence. But Ben still hankered for her and hoped that he would see her again for she had been, and still was, his idea of perfection.

He focused upon Ida and the present. 'I tell you that that was when he stepped over the line. We all knew it, but it was as if he did not care anymore.'

'What happened next?' Benjamin asked, wanting to know, but sure that it would upset him still further.

'They came for him at night. Folk was asleep and they brought a black cart all the way up here. It looked like the devil hisself had put it together. It had sides and a door at the back. You could lock folk up in it. Your pa put up a fight, but there were three of them onto one. The whole village was woken by the noise he made. They got him shackled and had him taken off.'

'The whole village was woken, yet no one helped him? You all stood by and let this happen?' Ben could hardly believe his ears.

'You don't understand, there was a doctor with them and a soldier. They declared that he was a lunatic on his own doorstep and then they hauled him off. He was to go to York asylum, God bless him, but after a week, they said he had calmed and he was said to have been moved to Gorebeck Asylum, which folk say ain't so bad. We heard that from Ethel who went there two weeks ago last Friday to sell her smoked herrings at the market. Her brother takes in the meat from the farm, over Beckton way, once a week. Anyhow, he also supplies the asylum and says that it is quite good, for a mad house, that is. Not that they have seen one before but folk say that them at York are made a spectacle of and that they would go mad if they were in there for more than a week, whether they was to start with or not. But I guess if you are out of your wits, you are not going to care what it's like, eh?' she asked him, and tried to smile to lighten her point, but they were ill chosen words said at the wrong time.

Ida's eyes were wide, staring at the speechless Benjamin who could barely take in what he was hearing. His pa had been declared mad, insane — a lunatic? How dare they incarcerate him? It was not to behold. It was nigh on impossible to imagine. Joseph Lamb was the most level headed person he had ever known; the man losing his mind was impossible to imagine. Benjamin remembered all the tales he had listened to of his life when he was at war. His father had seen men killed in front of him in the depth of a battle. His father had also told him how he had also witnessed the brutality of men at war, when their raised bloodlust was turned on the innocent victims left in the enemies' captured towns, no matter which side of the battle he was, the women, children and elderly would be left at their mercy. Sometimes they showed none. No, Benjamin knew his father had coped with too much horror in his life to be turned so easily in such a small village. If he was to have lost his sanity, surely it would have been then, or on his near return to England shortly afterwards, not when he was at home in his village, years later. He loved his job at the farm, but he was not in desperate need of it. He had made a profit from the battlefields of war, and had not come back poor. Something was totally wrong. His pa could turn his hand to anything, he would have found work somewhere else, so that was not the reason. Not during peacetime, not when there was every chance his son was still going to return to him. No, it was not right, he was a positive man and did not give in to black thoughts. He fought them until the light shone through again; it was Joe's way. There was something that had triggered his behaviour that people knew nothing of. Something had happened and it must be to do with the present owner of Marsh Hall. Someone had made a huge mistake; two huge mistakes, one by accusing his pa of being insane and the second by not bargaining on his son returning to rescue him. He stared at the woman opposite him.

'Ida, do not tell anyone I have returned here. I do not want word to reach Marsh Hall Farm or the asylum that Benjamin Lamb has returned before I have a chance to meet my father and find the truth out.' His father must have been ill, in body, but not in mind. If he behaved badly, then there had to be a reason for it, a fever perhaps, and Benjamin would be the one to discover what it was.

'Ida won't say a word, but you'll have to be gone before first light or you'll be seen for sure. Best put your horse round the back of the cottages. There is still a lean-to which will do for stabling it for a night. Here, you stay with Ida and catch your rest and I'll do it.' She stood up slowly and winked at him. 'No one will know you are here. My word, young Ben. I liked the old fool and I miss his wit and banter around the place. You rest then bring him back.'

Ben nodded and watched her go. There was no point him going to the hall to ask if they were responsible for putting his pa away. He must go to Gorebeck and rescue him. He would try visiting the man by entering through the front door to start with, but if that did not go well then he would use some of the skills he had learnt whilst at war. One way or another, his father would be free again and whatever demon had upset him would be laid to waste. First, though, he needed food, drink and a nap, then by the break of day he would go to Gorebeck Asylum, because there was none madder at that moment than the rage that filled Benjamin.

# 4

Teresa was woken up early the following morning as her maid barely knocked upon the door before bursting into her room. 'Miss Teresa! Miss Teresa, you are to rise and dress without delay. I have your tray and your travel clothes. You are to be going with your mama who is preparing to leave as we speak!' The maid rushed in, depositing a tray safely down upon the table, and then scurried over to the tall rectangular windows as she flung the long curtains open, flooding the room with early morning daylight. Teresa raised her head from her pillow. It was not like her to sleep in late. She stretched her arms out above the quilted covers and then slipped out of bed. Walking in her slippers she wandered over to the nearest window and stood to the side of the curtain, peering out. The street vendors below were only just setting out on their day. It was, she realised, still quite early. Teresa looked at the maid who was busy arranging Teresa's travelling clothes upon the end of her bed, ready for her to change into.

'Whatever is the matter, Peg?' she asked, as she took a sip from the warm milky chocolate drink which Cook had prepared for her. It was one of her favourites along with hot milk flavoured with the rich spice of nutmeg and the added sweetness of honey, when Cook had a ready supply of it.

'It is your mother, miss. She has decided that you need to take a journey to the market town of Gorebeck with her, as there is a particular establishment that she used to visit when you lived all the way up there, who, she believes, has some lovely accessories to match your dress for the dinner this Saturday evening.'

'Do I detect a note of disagreement with this, Peg?' Teresa asked, stifling a smile.

'Not for me to fathom it, miss. Not

my place. It is just . . . well . . . what I can't fathom is . . . ' She paused and disappeared for a moment into the cupboard before reappearing with Teresa's polished boots. 'No, it's not my place of course to express my opinion, but here we are in the city and your mother decides she knows a better place to go to buy your finery. Pardon me saying so,' she apologised and blushed, 'I thought we had the best shop establishments around these parts. Then what would I know?' She sniffed as she fussed about helping to make Teresa ready for her unexpected trip.

'It is quite alright, Peg. I can see why you might be perplexed, but perhaps what Mama is really doing is going on a social visit to spread her news to her friend who lives there and owns a milliners and haberdashery establishment, that we are receiving a guest this weekend, who she considers rather special. It is of no surprise to me. However, her early start is. She must be very excited about the forthcoming visit to plan such an expedition at short notice.' Teresa glanced out of the window, her enthusiasm waning as she realised the visit was going to be dull as she listened to her mama and Mrs Gregory swapping news and information upon Mr Brigton and his family.

Peg smiled at her, accepting her view of her mother's actions, but then added, 'Mr Johnston was called away last night, miss. I think that is when she made up her mind that now might be an opportune time to visit. He will be back the day after the morrow . . . late. You should see the list of preparations she has left us to do whilst you are away. All the things she wants finished and ready regarding the weekend visit. We will not be idle, that is for sure. I hope the young man is worth it . . . We could not be more pushed if the Prince Regent himself was arriving with his entire entourage.' Her hand shot up to cover her mouth. 'Sorry, I mean, of course he will be . . . and of course we shall have everything ready as your mama would rightly expect us to. Sorry for being so forward.' She fussed around.

'Peg, time will tell us if this man will be worth the high hopes that mama and Mr Johnston have of him. Do not worry that you have been open. We shall put it down to the suddenness of the news and no more than that. Best to keep your voice down, Mr Johnston would not approve if he heard me in such a discussion with my servant.'

Peg nodded.

Teresa moved over to the end of the bed and ran her finger along the lace cuff of the dress, before looking back at Peg. 'I do not suppose you know anything about him. I have been told a lot about his family and what they own, but nothing much about him — the man himself, that is: his looks or his character. If you have heard anything at all which could help me understand what I might expect . . . in confidence of course, I would treat it in a similar way,' she said quietly, and was intrigued when Peg's cheeks flushed slightly.

'Oh, miss, now you are asking me something. I would be in a lot of bother if I was caught filling your head with below stairs gossip . . . not that I am saying there is any regarding this young man. You know that Mr Johnston would turn me out without references and I would be in a right way, if that were to happen. Besides, it is maybe better that you should form your own opinion of this man and not rely on the opinions of others who have never met him and only heard rumours . . . ' her voice faded away as her face coloured and her eyes avoided Teresa's.

'What rumours?' Teresa asked, but Peg suddenly shot a look at the door.

'Is that the time? I must get on, or I shall be in trouble with Mrs Shellow. You know how she likes to keep a timely house. I will send young Millie in to help you dress.' As swiftly as she arrived she left in the same manner.

\*   \*   \*

Benjamin was early to rise and swift to eat his fish broth before mounting his horse and, under the cover of darkness, making his way across the tracks to the moor road avoiding the main villages. It was his intention to be at Gorebeck shortly after day break. Once there, he would watch the building first, see how it was situated and then decide how best to approach it. If he could smell or hear the asylum before he arrived then he would go to the gun makers and buy different supplies to the vitals he needed. He would have his father's liberty returned to him, one way or another.

Ida had been most insistent that no one could have helped him, but he found this hard to accept. Someone surely could have, if only they had asked questions or stood by the man. He had glowered at the church tower as he had passed by it. Another question he would ask was why had the good reverend not stood for his father's good name? Too many questions to ask, but no answers at the moment. He needed to ask the one man who could make sense of all of this — his father.

* * *

'Mama, it is unlike you to be so bold as to make such a decision to travel, especially on such a journey as this, on a whim.' Teresa sat within the carriage opposite her mother. This vehicle was her mother's pride. She could afford to travel within a carriage. Pride was a sin, but it was one of the few her mother had.

The coach had left the city walls behind and headed north up the old Roman road that would take them on to the market town of Gorebeck. It stood beyond the northern edge of the moors and was an important crossroads for the area.

'I want to see my good friend, Mrs Gregory. She has written to me telling me that she had some Belgian lace, which I think would look divine upon your dress. If not, it will keep for your next meeting with Mr Brigton. We have to plan ahead, Teresa. If he approves of you, then you will require more suitable attire. He will have to present you to his mama, and she will be looking for quality for her son and not a gold-digger. You must impress your humility upon her. When the time comes of course, we must not jump too far ahead but now is the time to have our plans in place. Mrs Gregory went to a ladies finishing school in Paris, she will be able to help you more than I on such issues. There was a time when she spent the season in London and even went into Almacks.'

'Almacks?' Teresa queried.

'You have a lot to learn, Teresa. There is time, as you have always been quick to take in knowledge, Teresa and now you will pick up some things which the Abbey school may have been remiss about.'

'Mama, can I ask you a question?' Teresa watched her mama snug under her blanket, and with her best aubergine velvet hat and coat on, she looked quite the lady.

'You just have, dear,' she quipped.

Teresa laughed. 'Another one, it relates to something you gave me a long time ago.' Teresa saw from the way her mother's eyes found hers that she was suspicious of what Teresa was referring to.

'What would that be? I believe I have given you a number of things over the years, Teresa.' Her voice was edgy.

'I want to know if you remember, when you were ill and before we moved away from our old home that you gave me a tin box and told me it was treasure?' Teresa saw her mother hesitate before replying.

'Why would you mention such a thing now?' Her manner was severe as soon as any connection with Alunby was made.

'I wondered if you remembered it.'

'I believe I was, or had been very ill and I asked you to go and bury it deep somewhere. You were always asking questions, never an easy child. I told you, you were far too young to understand.' Her mother was sitting straight backed. 'Tell me you did, for once, do as I requested.'

'Yes, I saw to it. You said that it was a treasure too complicated and precious for me to understand then. But I am grown now. So, Mama, what was in it that was so precious. Surely, I would understand now?' Teresa smiled, hoping that it would be infectious as her enthusiasm would also.

'That was treasure which should never see the light of day. It was something which was of your father and that is why I wanted it buried, like him, with his memory. I was too ill to see to it myself and that housekeeper was taking too many liberties, as she still does on occasion, with my things. What fanciful notions you had as a child, Teresa. I told you to bury my treasure as it was not for your young eyes. I was not giving you some great jewel of value. Whatever did you think in that mind of yours?' She shook her head and looked out of the window. 'Wherever you buried it, it will be no more than remnants now, as that is what happens to things when you bury them, they rot.' She sighed. 'See how your presence can dim the mood of a day! Do not do that to Mr Brigton. You keep your mind off the past and focus all your energy upon the present, that way you may have a more prestigious future.' She shook her head, and uttered, 'Treasure indeed!'

Teresa stared at the woman. Her own heart was sinking like the sun going down. Her words were sharp and unthinking. She had thought that tin held a secret, for her. A treasure between her mama and her that she would see revealed when she returned to her old home. Was she to believe that all her mama had been doing was using her to hide her own secrets away from Mr Johnston's hired housekeeper? She too stared out of the window; she swallowed trying to turn her own mood around. When she started to think, if that tin held a secret that needed hiding and it was too big a secret that she hid it from Mr Johnston, her own betrothed, then what was it that it held. Joe would be able to have dug deep, but he had always been a loyal friend to her and she was sure that he would have wrapped it well enough for her to preserve it for her return.

She smiled. There was treasure to be had, but it was going to be the sort that revealed a secret, and one she would unearth. She looked at the woman opposite and realised what a stranger she had become to her.

'That's better, Teresa, think only happy thoughts of your future and make this match happen. The past has gone. Leave it well behind you.'

# 5

Benjamin skirted the town of Gorebeck. From a distance he could see down through the trees that it was clearly important as a major cross-roads for the region. Funny, he thought, how he knew the name well enough, but as a child had not travelled more than to the towns along the bay. He stood, watching as a man who had travelled the world, yet was viewing Gorebeck for the first time. His experience from the wars had taught him what to look for to quickly assess an enemy's position, or an unfriendly township. If he wanted to break this one, he would blow the bridge after setting fires around the barracks, then pick off the enemy as they ran around within the confusion. However, this was a town at peace with the world around it, at least with the immediate one, yet within it; somewhere, his father was being kept a prisoner.

A stone bridge took the road over the river that looped around the town; it was obviously a place of growing importance. The houses at one end stood on either side of the river Gore. Fitting, he thought for a town with a barracks and an asylum, yet this place was changing from the remnants of a medieval market town to one with newer buildings. A row of fashionable terraced housing had been built along the far side of a newly laid road, which had its own raised walkway in front of their doors. Ladies could walk above the mud, whilst riders could dismount easily upon it.

The river swept away from the village behind the church, leaving the rest of the main road to lead toward a cobbled market square. This was where the roads crossed and took travellers either north towards Newcastle, south to Selby and York, west towards Harrogate or east in the direction of Whitby and the north east coast.

For a relatively small town it had at least four inns, the barracks were set beyond the market square, and the asylum was hidden away in a forested area between the town and the moors, toward the south. Realising this he made his way around the town, sticking to the edge of the forest which skirted the upper moor, slipping into the grounds surrounding the grey stone asylum building. His thoughts were dismal, his heart heavy, he wished he could blow a hole within the stark wall but knew that was the desperate thinking of a man confused, or rather a son in agony at the not knowing of what had become of his father. He was trained and disciplined. Benjamin Lamb swallowed his emotions and thought deeply. He needed to think through his actions before he put them into practice. If he was locked in gaol, who could help his father then? After sitting for a while and contemplating his best move, he headed back to the town, stabled his horse and took a room for the night at a respectable looking inn in the centre of the new street.

In his room he washed, shaved, rested for a couple of hours and laid out his good suit. He polished his boots, brushed down his jacket and waistcoat and then prepared a cravat. He intended to look respectable and would, hopefully, gain entry to his father without question. He then had another idea. Dressing quickly, he left the inn refreshed and headed to a shop which was in the middle of the town, in prime position. It was an establishment in two halves. One bay window was adorned with women's accessories, whilst the other sold bags, boots, belts, shavers and a myriad of items for gentlemen. He smiled as through one of the small window panes that made up this shop's frontage he spotted what he was looking for. He entered and smiled at the man behind the counter.

'Good day, sir,' he said politely as he glanced innocently around the room.

'Indeed, sir. If you should tell me what you seek I shall make it a better one still, I hope?'

Ben pointed to a black bag which was in the corner of the room, almost placed beyond view; it was the bag he wanted. At first sight it looked like one which a man of medicine would carry.

The man quickly walked over to it, raised it, giving it a quick wipe with his sleeve as he did to remove some dust. 'An excellent choice, sir!' He carried it over to the counter and carefully placed it down ready for him to inspect it.

Ben, looking doubtful, inspected it closely. 'It is used, sir,' he said, as if disappointed. However, a used bag would look less suspicious than a brand new one for the role he wanted to play to gain access to the asylum. After his incarceration in the French village where he was held captive, he knew something of places such as this one.

The thought of entering such a trap, knowingly, made his flesh prickle, picturing his father incarcerated in one made him feel nauseous.

The man shrugged his shoulder. 'It has had one previous owner, who left it behind at the inn some months back in part payment of his debts. I can tell you, honestly sir, that this is a strong case and has been bought by my good self as an investment for such a discernable gentleman as yourself. However, if you want a new valise, sir, I have an excellent tan one, well worth the extra cost I assure you . . . '

Ben offered the man half of what he felt the case would be worth, then haggled until he ended up paying two thirds of the price he was prepared to give for it. Happy that he had a good deal, he paid the eager clerk and carried it out in his hand. Having, he decided, wasted enough time, he was in a hurry to leave and act upon his plan.

★　★　★

The coach journey was quiet except for the rattle and jostle of the vehicle as it was pulled along well-worn tracks. Rather than risk upsetting her mother further, Teresa decided to watch the world go by in silence, whilst she planned how she would make her escape the moment Mr Brigton left them after his weekend visit. Her mother would be exhausted after entertaining such a high profile guest for so long, chaperoning and keeping up appearances, and would spend most of the first day in bed after the visit. Mr Johnston would have given so much of his time to his important visitor and would be keen to return to his business ventures, so then, Teresa decided, would be the best time to go for a ride which she would not return directly from. She would leave a note to say that she had worried incessantly over her uncle's health and the family estrangement and would return as soon as she had had her heart calmed of worry, knowing that all was well. They may disown her, but she doubted that as they wanted the match to Brigton's family too much. They would no doubt hide her absence, silence the servants and send a coach to fetch her back. Perhaps, Mr Johnston himself would come, then she would have her treasure or at least know the secret within it which might just give her some say in her own future at least. Clearly it disturbed her mama. Joe would explain all to her. She smiled, happily lost in her own plans when a stranger caught her eye as they approached the newly made walkway in the town's centre. Her mama was all attention as she looked for her friend's establishment. Seeing Teresa's smile she seemed to take this as a positive sign that her daughter shared her enthusiasm.

Benjamin strode purposefully along the walkway, a coach was approaching and slowing as it neared. He stepped slightly out of its way, so that the door could be opened by the driver as he jumped down. Ben glanced at the window of the coach from under his hat, with straight sides and narrow brim, like his trousers and greatcoat it accentuated his height and physical frame. He was transported back in time. He was no longer a gentleman in fine attire, but an ungainly lad leaning against a wall with a poorly crafted comb in his hand, made for his angel — one who was about to fly away and leave him. Despite his urgency and need to see his father, his feet stopped. Clearly in the window was the face framed by ash blonde locks, her eyes staring at him. A vision of his love, grown into the beauty he knew she would become.

He stood, bag in hand, as she disappeared from view for a moment. The mother, yes, that was her, unmistakable, older, but as unyielding a face as he had always remembered, alighted first, informing the driver to have her bags brought into the establishment Ben had just left. She could not wait, as her friend greeted her with open arms.

The two women bustled inside; the driver carried the bags behind after helping Miss Teresa out. The woman stopped and she hesitated, looking in his direction.

Benjamin took a step forward, and smiled.

'Sir, do I know you? Is it Benjamin? I . . . ' She hesitated, seemingly aware that they were momentarily alone.

'Miss Teresa . . . could it be anyone else?' He took a step forward, restraining the urge to fling his arms around her beauty and whisk her off her feet. He had found his angel again.

'Teresa!' her mother's voice beckoned her.

'I must talk to you, Ben. Not here. I need to find your father, I must visit him.'

'Teresa!' the voice sharpened.

Ben's spirits sank as he realised she must have heard about his father's plight also. Perhaps she would be the one to tell him the truth. 'If you know, you must tell me . . . '

'I must go.' She walked toward the shop. 'I shall see if I can slip out this evening,' she whispered, then smiled sweetly at him.

He continued on his way. Teresa had recognised him, but wanted to see his father. He was shamed that a tinge of jealousy swelled within his chest. He would help his father when he knew the truth and then he would see what Teresa knew of his fate. He walked towards the stables.

⋆   ⋆   ⋆

Teresa entered the establishment with her head held high.

'You are such a beauty, Teresa. Your mama has told me the good news. Soon your future will be secure. Come! Come! We must take tea. Cynthia! A tray . . . Please come into my home. George and Emma shall see to things here. We shall go to my new house. You will have passed it by as you pulled up.' The woman glowed with pride as her maid ran ahead of them to her new terraced house.

Teresa could only think of the sighting of Benjamin. How strange that he should be here. Now she was sure she was meant to go to Alunby. He looked like a doctor or surgeon or something. How could he be so? Whatever fortune had given him for a life opportunity she knew that her Benjamin would help her, he always did. Benjamin was a reliable and solid type, just like his father. Perhaps he was a surgeon or doctor's helper. That would be it. What had he meant, though? Surely he had not been a party to her secret. What else was there for her to know about? She would find out soon enough when they met. He looked at her with those same soft eyes her old spaniel used to. What a good friend he had been and would be again. When she discovered the secret, she would, if there was any treasure in it to be had, reward both him and his father for being so loyal to her. Her mother often moaned that good servants were hard to come by, yet the woman had left two excellent ones in Alunby years earlier. Teresa was learning just how blinkered her mama's eyes were, unlike her own.

# 6

Ben tried to put this unexpected meeting from his mind. He must go to the asylum. He was dressed, he had his bag and had to think as a medical man — he had seen enough of them over the last few years, genuinely caring men who were often saddened by their lack of ability to save life in the field to evil blackguards who cared only for their own skin. A ship's surgeon he met on his initial journey out to Oporto had told him that he had studied for all of six weeks before embarking. It was with little wonder that he had tried to treat a man who had just lost a leg after a few days of agony, the poor man lost his life also. The surgeon, woefully inept, drank his conscience away.

Ben made his way toward the archway, situated mid terrace, that allowed the coaches to go through to the stabling and an old inn hidden well behind this new façade of housing. He stopped as Miss Teresa's carriage was taken slowly past him by the driver, through the archway. How much time had passed, he mused, since that day when, dejected, he had waved farewell to his dream girl, his friend and, he had presumed, his love? Now she was a beautiful young woman and he a man grown; yet somehow, looking at the coach as it passed him by, the void between them seemed as big a chasm as ever. He glanced back to the shop. He could not be as bold as to walk in and demand to talk to her in private. What would he do — reminisce about their childhood and all the antics they had enjoyed together, his love of the outdoors and her daring to try and keep up with him? How he loved that spirit of hers. Or forget niceties and simply ask her directly what she knew of his father's circumstances?

Ben had to think clearly. He had to

think like a skirmisher, a trained soldier, like the officer he had fought tooth and nail to become, respected and positioned, and not like an emotional lad whose pulse skipped a beat every time he saw his heart's desire. He mulled over his thoughts. It had been years since they parted, the hurt had slowly dissipated, memories forgotten. Why then, had one quick glance of Teresa's beautiful face, a chance meeting and a few words of greeting set that same pulse racing like no other wench he had ever known?

He clenched his fist around the handle of his bag and walked at a pace to the stables where his horse was stalled. He was a man now and not a misty-eyed boy, Captain Benjamin Lamb, a man who had climbed from lieutenant and made a life for himself, and the fate of another, Mr Joseph Lamb, his father, rested within his hands. If he could not control his senses then it could well result in one 'Lamb' being led to the slaughter.

\* \* \*

'Who is that fine looking young man?' Cynthia asked Teresa.

Teresa's mother looked at her and then around as Benjamin was just stepping out of sight.

'How would Teresa know such a thing? We have just arrived. I have no idea, Cynthia. I presumed he was the local doctor.' She glanced at Teresa who shrugged her shoulders gently.

Cynthia smiled. 'My dear friend, if he were our local doctor, I think the ladies of this town would be having the vapours at a frequent rate!' Cynthia giggled at her own quip.

Teresa laughed, but her mama cast a cursory look at her whilst acknowledging her friend's wit. They arrived at the door of Cynthia's new property and were shown in by the maid who had gone on ahead. She saw them to a room and then disappeared back to the rear of the property where the kitchens were situated, leaving the ladies to enjoy tea within the comfort of a parlour. The high window had a good vantage overlooking the road, church and the distant bridge over the river. The main interest to Cynthia, Teresa assumed, was who would be coming and going along the road. Taking in her sumptuous surroundings, Teresa could only assume that her business must be very profitable.

Teresa was quick to make use of the window seat as the two ladies sat in the rosewood chairs around a matching rosewood drum table, newly laid with a pot of fresh tea and perfectly round tea bowls. Cynthia showed her skill at pouring and serving her guests. Whilst the fluid cooled they chatted of Teresa's future prospect.

'Yes, Cynthia, Mr Brigton, the only son of 'Brigton's of Hewerton' and the most eligible man in the area!' Her head bobbed with the enthusiasm of her words.

Cynthia, Teresa noted, did not respond as eagerly as her mama had expected.

'Mr Wilfred Graham Bernard Brigton, you refer to?' Cynthia asked.

'Yes! Yes, the very one! The heir to their whole estate. Actually, I should say their growing estates as they have recently purchased land next to a canal somewhere south to build another manufactory! Is it not splendid news?' her mother spoke, and was all animated in her joyful state.

Cynthia patted her friend's hand and then whispered something in a lowered tone. Teresa avoided turning her head to blatantly ask what it was that had been said between these two matriarchal women, but listened intensely trying to understand what it was that was being spoken between them as she peered out of the window.

'Teresa, dear.' Her mother cut across her thoughts and, Teresa noted, was acting suspiciously. She had obviously silenced her friend.

'Yes, Mama,' she said sweetly, not wanting to take her attention away from the view outside the house for long in case Benjamin returned to the area. For some reason she felt a desperate yearning to speak to him again. Of course it was to see Joe, but beyond her immediate yearning lay another strange and deeper one.

'Please, be a dear. Will you pop back to the shop for me? I am sure I have left my gloves in there, by the table.' She smiled, but her eyes were not as happy as when she had first arrived, or as she told her friend the match she proposed for her daughter. Something Cynthia was about to say to her, or had inferred, had suppressed her mother's high spirits.

'No, Mama, you did not,' Teresa answered, thinking quickly.

'I think I did. Please go and look for them!' She widened her eyes slightly in her daughter's direction, telling her plainly she wished her to leave for a few moments.

'Yes, Mama, I am certain. However, I think I saw them on the seat of the carriage.' She stood and walked over to the door. Her mother looked a little anxious.

'Go to the corner of the archway and see if you can see Belson, but do not venture beyond the pathway, Teresa. Remember this is a civilised town and you cannot go venturing around the stables. You must protect your reputation, particularly at this delicate time. Hurry, for I shall fret if you take more than a few moments!' Her words seemed genuinely meant.

'Of course, Mama, I shall see if Belson is to be seen and if not I shall check quickly at the shop, but will return straight away if not.' She did not wait for a reply. Teresa left the room and slipped her travel coat back on and made her way out of the front door, down the two steps and walked along the raised pathway toward the archway. She had reached the edge of the pavement when she heard a horse approaching. The face who peered down at her as it stopped in front of her looked as surprised and bewildered as her own.

'It is really you . . . you look a deal different, Miss T.'

He seemed pleased when she smiled at his pet name for her. He had tired early of forever calling her Miss Teresa as they ran wild in the dunes. So to him, she had become 'Misty'.

'Ben, you are a gentleman now. How well you have fared in life. Are you a surgeon or his assistant?' she asked, but saw a cloud dull the joy in his eyes when she posed her question.

'Do I look like a butcher of men?' he asked abruptly.

She was taken by surprise. 'Sir, I said a surgeon, not a butcher. I would have asked if you were a doctor or a physician, but know that would be impossible and I did not wish to insult you, Ben.' She looked at him with wide innocent eyes and she saw a faint flush of his cheeks, which told her he still was as easy to control or 'mistify' as he always had been as a child. Remembering her time limitation as her mother would be awaiting her return, she looked at him earnestly. 'I need to talk to your father, Ben. Can you escort me to Alunby? It is important.'

He leaned over toward her, crossing one arm over his saddle. 'Why do you need to see my father if you believe him to still be Alunby?' He looked at her as if he was trying to peer into her soul.

'Where else would he be?' She was confused. Ben, her Ben, was looking almost angry. 'What have I said to upset you, Ben?'

'I am troubled, Misty, but not by you. My father is here in Alunby and I also need to see him.'

'If he is here, then that is excellent. We can see him together. I will have to leave you now, as I am expected back in minutes, but I can return later. Mama always takes a nap before dinner, so then would be a good time for me to slip away. I am sure I will be able to work this out, somehow. Where do you live? Does your father work here? Tell me, Ben, for it is important. I can explain later, but you must see that my need is great and I will only be here for two nights. I may need one of you to take me back to Alunby. Ben . . . Ben, what is wrong? I can explain later.' Teresa could see that he was staring at her blankly . . . strangely.

'Meet me at the hour of four in the church, and then I shall explain to you what the situation is. Then you can tell me why you wish to see my father so urgently, when you believe him to still reside in Alunby. You have not kept in touch with him, so do not know his circumstance.' He paused for a moment.

'He is my friend, Ben, as you are. Why would I imagine either of you had left Alunby?' She looked at him, knowing her words only seemed to make things worse between them, but not knowing why.

'Do you think that whilst your life moves on, ours has not? Do you think that your friends do not have need to live a life also, or do we sit on our stools and wait for you to remember us?' His words were almost bitter.

Teresa swallowed and took a step back away from this stranger, who said words to her, the truth of which stung her heart. 'I am sorry you feel that way. I . . . ' she felt unequal to the task of explaining her meaning.

'I shall be inside that church at four o'clock.' He nodded toward the Norman building. 'I hope to have the answer to some of my own questions by then. If our friendship ever meant anything to you, Miss Teresa, you be there and I shall listen to your problems and answer what questions I can. Then we will speak of my father.' He walked the horse forward.

'What if I cannot be there at four o'clock, Benjamin?' she asked politely and saw him turn his head back to look at her. Something inside her stirred, she felt her cheeks warm and her heartbeat quicken. Was she frightened of the man her Ben had become? No, far from it, what she felt was not fear, it was excitement. It was something new to her, a feeling she had not experienced since she was a child who ran the dunes wild with her friend, the odd-job man's son. It was a connection that she did not understand and could only put it down to her pleasure at seeing Joe's son again and knowing her quest would soon be accomplished. Therefore, the treasure was coming nearer to her; it was a sign that she should follow her instincts and seek it out. Ben had been put in her path for her to achieve her goal. It was meant to be. No wonder she was excited. 'You'll be there,' he said simply, and rode off.

Teresa watched him, with a smile slowly growing across her face. He sensed it too.

# 7

Teresa returned to the house having quickly popped into the shop only to show her face to those trusted by Cynthia to look after it in her absence, as she already knew that the gloves would not be there. She had been sent on a fool's errand as her mama would send her when she was a child, to occupy her whilst her mama gossiped with her guests, few though they had been. Perhaps that was why her mother guarded them jealously, not wanting Teresa to share. She also realised that their driver would be within the inn, imbibing of ale, no doubt. Therefore, knowing full well there was no point to her looking for him, her errand had been seen to be completed as best it could be.

She re-entered the house. The housemaid took her coat and hat from her again, so that Teresa returned to the parlour. Her mother, she thought, looked quite pale.

'I am sorry, Mama. I could not find the gloves in the shop and there was no sign of our driver outside that I could see from the walkway.' She sat at the tea table and sipped her now cooled tea. It had a delicate flavour, which refreshed her palate. Like the porcelain that held it, it was of excellent quality; she said as much to her mother's friend.

'Teresa, the gloves are of no importance. However, I feel that I must take my rest now, the journey has been quite arduous and we must not keep Cynthia from her previously arranged appointments. We shall wash and rest so that we are fresh for dinner.' Her mother stood up.

Teresa was hungry and looked longingly at the platter in the centre of the table, which had a few delicate cakes and pastries left upon it.

Cynthia intervened on her behalf. 'Why don't you go on upstairs? I shall send my maid to you with some fresh scented water and a towel and, once Teresa has had chance to satisfy her appetite, she will follow, won't you, dear?' She looked at Teresa.

'If that is acceptable, Mama? I am a little peckish.' She tried to sound innocent and not desperate to gorge herself as she was very hungry.

'Very well. When you are ready, dear.' She left the room, Cynthia followed, summoning her housemaid as she did.

Teresa tucked in to the pastry that had taken her eye when she had sat down. She was wiping a crumb from the corner of her mouth with the napkin when Cynthia returned to her.

She leaned forward intending to stand up, and politely excuse herself. 'Thank you, that was delightful. I shall keep Mama company for a while.'

'Please, stay with me awhile, Teresa. I would like to talk to you. Come and sit with me.' She perched herself on the window seat and waited for Teresa to obey her.

'Thank you, the tea was lovely . . . You have a lovely home,' Teresa began to speak, wondering what they would find to talk about, or if this was some sort of test of her social skills. Hadn't her mother told her that this lady could school her in the delicate ways of behaviour within society? Her own were very lacking. Her 'schooling' had been limited, her visits had been relatively few and her mother had little conversation at the best of times.

'Yes, I do. But that is not what I wish to talk to you about. Tell me first, who was the man who you spoke to when you alighted from the coach?'

Teresa realised that whilst her mother's back had been to her as she scurried to meet her friend, Cynthia had been watching them from the window and had seen her talking briefly to Ben. 'He seemed to think he recognised me from somewhere. I told him I am not from this town. I presumed, like Mama, that he was a local medical man.' Teresa, convincing herself that she was speaking a near truth, looked at Cynthia meeting her eye level.

'Tell me then, what you think of Mr Brigton?' Cynthia stared back at her.

Teresa sat down and answered honestly this time. 'I do not think anything of him in particular, because we have not met and I have decided not to judge the man until I have been introduced and spent some time in conversation with him. Besides, he may not find me to his liking,' she said politely.

'I can assure you he will.'

'I do not think so. You see my education in society is limited and I fear I may not be refined enough for his taste. I do not play an instrument at all.' Teresa realised that she had not been concerned about this meeting for she was convinced the man could 'buy' himself a higher born bride than she was.

Cynthia's reaction was to smile. 'You do not seem disappointed at the thought of rejection, Teresa. Could it be you are not for the match?' There was a slight conspirational tone to her voice.

'I have not met him, so I cannot say as he is only the first one who may be interested.'

Cynthia's eyes were a chestnut hue, which matched her hair, although the latter was now starting to fade to grey. Her head was held high and her hair swept up atop it. 'He needs to find a wife, my girl, one who can provide him heirs to satisfy his father. He . . . will not inherit if he does not produce sons before his father passes away. You see he has every reason to look for a pretty and healthy young woman, regardless of if she can play pianoforte. You can always be taught that whilst you are confined.'

Teresa swallowed, realising the seriousness of her situation. She had been so engrossed in plotting to recover the hidden secrets of the lost treasure that she had been remiss regarding what was really happening around her. If this match was rushed through, her future would be determined and sealed. In a moment of revelation she now understood that whilst she had been thinking selfishly as a child obsessed on their own course, her world could change around her thrusting her into the role of wife to a complete stranger. Her mind flitted to Benjamin; she might need his help for a different reason. He might know of this man. 'I do not think I would want to marry and have children straight away. I am quite young still and . . . '

Cynthia raised a hand in a gentle gesture to silence her. 'My dear, whether you want children or not, believe me when I tell you, you will be given them.' She flushed slightly; Teresa wanted to smile, she knew how men gave women babies because she had seen one of her friends at the school having a liaison with the curate's son. Teresa had returned unexpectedly to their room and discovered the two of them, naked and wrapped around each other. The scene was shocking and comical at the same time. After James had left, Isabelle explained all to her friend, but the two were deeply in love. Teresa had been told of their antics and all had been a shockingly shameful private joke, until Isabelle had fallen with child and the lad had felt the stick of his own father, before the engagement was announced and the marriage soon after. But they were in love. Teresa was to be seen as an innocent, it was expected and it was her screen, because then no one would suspect she was capable of defying her mother and leaving to seek her treasure out. She subdued a smile, realising that now that goal would not involve so many problems, if only Ben would help her and take her to Joe.

Cynthia cleared her throat. 'My friend, Mrs Forthingworth, who lives near their Harrogate estate, knows the family well. He is looking for a young, healthy, woman who is beautiful and who will come with a respectable dowry. You, my dear, fit his needs very well. I also know that his father is not in good health and therefore the young Mr Brigton needs to find this paragon of virtue sooner rather than later. You will, I expect, spend your first season coming out with a man firmly attached to your side. That is, if he cannot arrange a wedding post haste, so he will be free to party the season away, as is his usual habit knowing that he has made his catch.' Cynthia added a gesture of a raised brow as if to emphasize her point.

'If you will excuse my being blunt, Mrs . . . '

'Cynthia, please. Between us we can be informal, are we not friends, Teresa?' she asked.

'Yes, if you wish it to be so, but not in front of Mama. She likes formalities to be kept and would consider that familiarity to be disrespectful . . . You do not seem to hold the man in high esteem. Has he been offensive in some way to your friend? Or, does she, perhaps, have an eligible daughter to marry off herself?' This last comment brought a glint of humour to Cynthia's eyes.

'Well, well, my new young friend is not as green as cabbage looking! I am impressed Teresa. I always suspected that behind those big innocent eyes of yours lay a very active mind. No, my dear, she has only sons and all blessedly married. Your mama does not seem to hear my words; the truth is something she hides from. No please do not take offence . . . I know your mama well and I love her despite her failings as she does me, but I will say something to you, perhaps against her will, but I think it is necessary for you to understand that it is you who will hold the initial power in this match. Take care with this man. He has a reputation for placing ladies in difficult 'positions', should we say. He has taken liberties and spoilt the future worth of some silly young girls already, three I believe, ruining their good names with his coercive ways; ones who he had no intention of becoming engaged to. He may be different with you, until you are wed, if his need to be married is great, although if he did claim you the marriage would be set on his terms. He is no romantic hero from a novella, my dear. He is a man of the world and it would do you well to act as though you were perhaps more worldly than you are. Keep him at a distance until you are assured of the wedding ring and of his fortune. Once he announces the engagement, still play the coy little dove. You want that wedding ring upon your finger and the wedding announced to the civilised world before you allow him any of your favours. Let him sow his seed and give you children once you are Mrs Brigton. When that is done, then he can scatter it elsewhere if he must, if you will pardon the phrase, or wherever he chooses once the heir and the spare is there. You will then be able to enjoy spending the family fortune and learning the pianoforte if you wish.

He is said to be most generous.' Cynthia let out a long breath as if she had been desperate to say all, before allowing Teresa to comment.

'What of love? Does that not count for anything in this match, Cynthia?' Teresa asked, not knowing why, but it suddenly meant everything to her. She was not going to be used and discarded just to provide a man with sons. It sounded cold and impersonal on this the most personal of issues.

'My dear girl, love your children. If you are fortunate, whilst you have your looks you may well find that you can tame him. It might be possible. Rogues have changed before, but better to enter such an arrangement knowing the truth of it, rather than have false dreams shattered. I wish you well.' After departing this wisdom, she patted Teresa's hand and stood up. 'Now, you go to your mama, a little wiser I hope, and I will see you both at dinner.'

'Thank you, Cynthia, for your honesty,' Teresa said with surprising sincerity, for she now understood the danger.

'You are my guest. It is the least I can do. Enjoy your rest. We shall talk more with your mama this evening and I shall find out what the upright and honest Mr Johnston has been doing of late.' She winked back at Teresa before she left.

Teresa waited a few moments to gather her thoughts together. She strongly suspected Cynthia would already know what anyone who crossed her path was doing, so why refer to Mr Johnston in such a way? She had better be careful that she did not make her mama suspicious of her new knowledge or when she slipped out to meet Ben at four o'clock. It was clear that Cynthia was already curious about him.

* * *

Ben rode at a pace until he passed through the gates to the asylum. Here he composed himself and walked the horse down the drive and up to the steps in front of the large black double doors. He dismounted, looping the reins securely onto a metal hoop secured in the ground. Ben could hear sounds from inside, but no awful pitying screams. He breathed deeply, he felt sick in the pit of his stomach, hating the memories of confinement this place brought back to him. But this may not be a gaol, it was no Bedlam either, there were no wailing cries, no odious odours to greet him and the outside of the building was in good repair.

He lifted the wrought iron door-knocker in the shape of a lion's head and let it clang down. It was not long before the door was opened wide. Inside, the entrance hall's stone walls were painted white. The floor was chequered with large black and white squared tiles. A woman stood the other side of the door in a long pale green dress over which she wore a white apron with a grey cloth hat atop her head restraining her hair.

'Yes, can I help you, sir?' she asked Ben.

'I am here to see a Mr Joseph Lamb.' He could see a large stone staircase that led up to different floors opposite.

'Oh,' she looked at his bag and smiled, 'Doctor, we did not send for you. We have our own doctor in charge here. There would be no need. Besides, he is settled now.' She moved the door as if to close it. Ben put a hand firmly against it moving it further open.

'You do not understand. I am here to see him on behalf of his son.' He stepped inside, uninvited.

'The master, Dr Gregory, is not here at present.' She looked a little anxious.

'I did not come here to see Dr Gregory. I came to see Mr Lamb, then I will make an appointment to see Dr Gregory.' He smiled, trying to restrain the desperate emotions welling within him.

She looked uncertain.

'When I have seen Mr Lamb, I will

then be in a position to talk about his situation earnestly to Dr Gregory. I have travelled a long way, miss, all the way from London.'

'London!' she repeated, her eyes widened.

'Yes, Mr Lamb is not without friends, miss.' He left the words hanging, not wanting to scare her off, but desperate to press his point.

She smiled. 'Of course, Joe . . . Mr Lamb will have friends.' She shut the door. 'I will take you to him and then get you an appointment to speak with Dr Gregory, but you must not upset him. He is fine when he can work peacefully, but don't go upsetting him. Best not mention his son . . . yet . . . Not until you have spoken to Dr Gregory. The mention of his name really upsets him.' She gestured he should follow her, which he did gladly.

Instead of being led up the stairs to the 'confinement rooms' as she described them, he was walked along a corridor which ended at the back of the building, leading to a walled garden at the rear. Near the corner of this vast space at the furthest point away from the building was an outhouse. The garden was well tended, with vegetable and herb gardens. Some pigs were penned in the opposite far corner. The place seemed quite tranquil. Even a cluster of apple trees provided shelter under which a bench had been placed.

The woman stopped a few feet from the outhouse. 'Joe, I have a visitor for thee, all the way from London.'

'Tell them to go back there then,' came the sarcastic reply.

Ben found he smiled instantly, but hearing the man's voice again made him swallow back a wave of emotion.

'That's not friendly, Joe.' She stood by the doorway and a figure appeared at the other side. Ben had tipped his hat forward slightly so that the shadow of the sun on his brim would obscure his face.

'Are you going to be nice to Doctor . . . ?' She looked back as she realised she did not even know his name.

Ben thought quickly. 'Dr Benson,' he said quietly.

'Joe, are you going to be nice to Dr Benson?' she asked. 'He has travelled a long way.'

'Very well.' The shadow disappeared back inside the outhouse.

The woman turned to Ben. 'You can go in now. But if he shows agitation and starts sobbing, leave quickly. He can be violent, but has not been for some time now.' She smiled and left him alone looking at the outhouse. Tentatively, he stepped forward until he was in the doorway. Ben put down the bag and stepped into the half-light inside.

His father was sitting, just as he used to, on a stool with a chisel in one hand and a small mallet in the other as he worked at fixing some broken object.

'Well, doctor, put your potions aside, for I'll take none. Say your business and leave!' He looked up.

Ben slowly removed his hat and

propped it on top of the discarded bag. He then came a pace nearer his father. 'Pa . . . Pa what happened?'

His father's tired eyes squinted and focused on his son's face. He looked shocked, the chisel fell from his hand, but the mallet was still raised. 'Ben, is it really you?' his voice cracked with emotion as he uttered the words.

Ben stepped forward. 'Yes, it is!'

The tears flowed freely, the man stepped forward. 'You!' he muttered as he rushed forward.

Ben opened his arms, but the mallet was still raised high.

# 8

Teresa opened the door quietly so as not to disturb her mama who appeared to be sleeping.

'What took you so long, Teresa? I hope you were not listening to idle gossip or over indulging. You need to be careful of your complexion now. Cynthia has her fanciful notions, she will be able to show you how to behave, but when one is with her informally she forgets herself. Although, I know she means no harm. I think it is the drawback of her having to find her own means to live. We are lucky; Mr Johnston provides for our needs, she has to earn her own money through her shop. If her husband had left her better provided for she would not have had to sully her good name with opening a shopping establishment.'

These words were spoken as her

mother rested upon the bed. She had washed and taken off her shoes, then lain down.

Teresa entered the room, closing the door quietly behind her, but was thoughtful and did not speak. Her head was filled with Cynthia's words of the man she was being handed over to, for that was what it felt like. She looked at her mother, then shivered as a horrible thought crossed her mind; what if she were entering a room where a man who was as a stranger to her was resting, or waiting for her presence, how would she behave? What would she do if she did not even like that man? From what she had been told it was quite possible that she would not. What then? He would have all the legal right of it and she none. She imagined her Ben. That was how she had always thought of him — 'her Ben'. She had never given a thought for how he would feel when she left. He still liked her; she sensed that, she was still his 'Misty' whoever that was. The way he had said the word, held warmth and something more, yet all she had thought about was how he could lead her to his father and a childhood dream of treasure.

'Teresa! Are you listening to me, girl, or do I bore you?' her mama snapped.

'No, I was just thinking that perhaps it was the money her husband left her which had paid for the shop and this splendid house,' Teresa replied, without thinking that perhaps her words were nearer the truth than her mama cared to hear.

'You are becoming quite an opinion-ated young woman,' her mama lowered her voice, but it did not lose any of the vexed attitude within it, 'If he left her so well cared for, then it is sheer greed that she should seek to make more of it. It is not as if she has any children to leave it to! This is not a characteristic which is at all admirable or sought in a young lady. It is for men to provide for us.'

Teresa looked at the woman on the bed, wondering how she ever managed to think that she may be pining for her daughter when they were apart; she had a heart that was totally self absorbed.

'Mama, tell me what you think Mr Brigton will be like?' Teresa hoped that she would pass on some words of care or advice as Cynthia had done.

'I told you. He is set to inherit a fortune. He will provide for all of your needs and you will make Mr Johnston and me very proud. I should imagine we will be able to visit their London residence in the summer, though I dread the thought of the journey.' She closed her eyes again. 'I shall have to have new dresses also. It will take time to plan, but we must appear worthy.'

'But what is the man like? Do you know if he is handsome, generous of spirit, caring, cultured, or a man of sporting achievement?' Teresa also kept her voice low.

'He is rich, or will be soon enough. All you have to do is please him. That surely cannot be beyond you? Just be polite, keep your opinions to yourself, support his and charm his mother.

Apparently she holds strong influence over the father. I have heard that it is her doing that the son must marry to gain his inheritance. She shows sense and strength. Perhaps you will learn from her. Now, I tire, wash and be quiet, I must sleep before we dine later or I will not be wakeful enough to keep up with Cynthia's banter.'

Teresa stared at her for a moment before pouring herself some fresh water from the pitcher. Her own mama cared not if she should be happy, so long as she was rich. Teresa washed her tears away and decided she would seek her own happiness elsewhere. She would ask Ben, he would know what to do for the best, he always had.

\* \* \*

'Father!' Ben snapped and grabbed the mallet from his father's hand as the older man had raised it high. His eyes betrayed his inner turmoil and indecision. His arm fell to his side as the mallet was dropped to the floor. Ben hugged him closely to his body. His father seemed smaller in frame. Ben tried to stop his own tears rolling from the corners of his eyes as the man sobbed in his arms. It was some moments before those same arms held the son in a return gesture. Then the sobs abated.

'What have they done to you, Pa? Why are you here?' Ben held his father at arm's length, supporting his unsteady frame.

His father's face stared into his own. 'Not them, Ben, you!'

'Me?' Ben released him. 'Why? I sent letters to Marsh Farm Hall for you, but Ida said you never received them. She inferred that Colonel Mathews' brother was less than an honourable man . . . ' He paused as he saw his father's eyes harden once more.

'Runs in the family.' He looked away.

Benjamin was confused. His father had always spoken highly of the colonel. He had been raised on tales of their exploits, daring attacks, near death and capture and the harshness of army life. Yet here he was belying their family name. Why?

'Pa, I was a prisoner of the French for nearly two years. If I had not been an officer I would not be returning to you at all. I could not get back to you before my journey to Alunby. Then I discover you are in this place. Why? I had no idea what was happening, and still I do not understand. Why are you here? Surely you did not think I would not return. You of all people always taught me not to give up. How can I have had anything to do with your circumstances? What lies have you been told?' His father rested against a work table, 'Not you directly, but . . . ' Joe folded his arms in front of his body, not in defiance but as if hugging himself. 'I cannot begin to explain to you . . . I am so glad you are well . . . but . . . I . . . You had better leave. I will stay here, I care for nothing anymore.'

'Pa, we've always been close, you and

I, no secrets, remember? You told me . . . ' Ben watched as his father's fist clenched, the knuckles turning white. 'Pa? Whatever it is you must tell me, or I will not be able to help you.'

His father's eyes focused on his. 'I never saw it in you before. Never wondered why you are so tall and I stocky. Why you should be clever and quick and me just good with my hands; handy to have at your side in battle, loyal and good to pick up after him, but I never saw him in you.'

'Pa, this is nonsense you speak. You must be confused. I am taking you out of here. What have they done to you?' Ben leaned over to pick up his father's old coat from the hook on the wall, when Joe's hand grabbed his arm.

'Even when the money was left as a 'Thank you' — a thank you to me, for my loyalty for my 'services', to provide a lieutenant's commission for 'my' son. I still never saw it. How foolish Joe Lamb was. How trusting . . . ' Tears flowed down his cheeks, 'How proud I was of 'my son', my only child.'

Benjamin felt empty inside. He was quick-witted enough to know that what his pa was saying inferred a terrible truth, but he could not fathom why his father should doubt his own son's birth. 'Pa, I am your son. You helped mother give birth to me, you told me that, I can be no other. Who has placed these thoughts in your head and why?'

'They are not just thoughts, lad. They were written down.' Joe stared at him, looking him square in the eye for the first time since he had arrived. He wiped away the moisture from his eyes.

'You cannot read.' Ben did not say it harshly as he had no wish to make him feel even less than he already was. He was grabbing at straws. He knew he had to persuade him that he believed a nightmare, living an untruth.

'No, I can't, but I took the letter to a man who could; a trusted friend, someone who would tell me honestly upon the Holy Book, in confidence, what it said.

'He was a priest. You took it to the church and what this letter said made you angry. Is that the way it happened? You would not believe the man?' Ben was starting to understand something of what Ida had told him.

'I threw the Holy Book across the church. I stormed to the hall knowing he was not there. The Colonel died in my arms and I hope now he has gone to hell!' He was standing up now almost shouting at Ben.

'Colonel Mathews, you always spoke so highly of him. How can you hate him so? What did the letter say? How did you come by it? Who gave it to you? Pa, you are my pa, no one else could measure up to you. I will have no other no matter what a piece of paper tells me. No one will ever matter more than you to me. Where is it now, this letter?' Ben was holding his father's arms and staring straight into his eyes. 'You . . . You are my pa!'

The cloud of anger dispersed from Joe's eyes, as he spoke gentler this time.

'Ben, I brought you up. Perhaps even dragged you up, but you are not my blood son. He wrote a letter of confession for his own wife, in case he was killed in the field. How thoughtful of him, eh? The widow, left alone for years in his family's home, only the staff and his overseer Mr Johnston to help run the estate, to be sent a letter to ease his conscience. 'His conscience' — I don't think he knew what one was. He wished to make things right by you 'YOU!' It was I who carried his pack, tended his wounds, made his tent, and supplied my wife when he was worse for drink. He slept with her. Her illness; it was all caused by him . . .'

Ben buried the hurt he felt deep inside. She had died giving life to him. He thought it was his fault if anyone's, but for his father to be so torn over this loss again was heartbreaking to both.

'Father, where is this letter? Who gave it to you?' He held the man firmly, but in a supportive not angry manner, for in his heart he cared for no other as his father.

'Miss Teresa . . . ' Joe looked at him. 'Her treasure, I stole it and it nearly destroyed me.'

★   ★   ★

Teresa finished refreshing herself and then rested in a chair reading quietly until she was sure her mama slept. It was nearly a half hour past three o'clock. Quietly, she placed the book down and then slipped out of the room across the landing and tiptoed silently down the carpeted stairs.

The maid had just crossed from the parlour to the back rooms of the house. Teresa froze, waiting for her to pass before continuing down to collect her coat, hat and gloves. She was trying to calm her nerves. What she would say if she was seen, she had no idea. Slipping out of the doorway and down the two steps, she turned to her left and kept as near as she could to the buildings, in case Cynthia should look out from her bay windowed shop. Teresa decided this was highly unlikely, but better safe than sorry. Something in those words did not ring true. She had an awful feeling that her plans were becoming unravelled, poor as they were, with each minute. At the point of the archway she almost ran down the step, across the cobbled stones and up onto the other side of the terrace. Once she had reached the end, it would be just a matter of crossing the bridge and slipping through the church's graveyard and into the building itself. If the vicar appeared she would ask if she could sit in silence for a time. How bad would that be, to hide the truth from a priest? Still, she reasoned that as she was being guided towards Ben, Joe and her secret treasure, she was certain no harm would be done by such a slight subterfuge.

★ ★ ★

It was now Ben's turn to sit on the stool, his head held momentarily in his hands. Suddenly he ruffled his hair, stood to his full height and placed his hat upon his head, collecting the bag in his hands.

'Father, we cannot sort this out here. By whose authority are you kept here? Tell me and I will challenge it.'

Joe laughed. 'Oh Ben, no one keeps me here. I choose to stay, where I can work in peace, away from all of it. With you taken from me, my job . . . my workroom gone, my memories defiled, what is there for me in Alunby? Do you think I want to return to where I will be treated as 'Mad Joe' the man who lost his dignity, went wild in such a small town, a reputation destroyed and was hauled off to the asylum? You have it all wrong, lad. Initially I was taken to the York institution.' Joe paused and shook his head. 'Hell on earth that was, and I have seen hell before. Fortunately, the good Dr Hazelmere, who runs this establishment, was there seeing a patient he was going to bring here. He examined me. Instead of being committed I was brought here for observation. Well, he observed me and gave me this place to use. Joe can fix things again. I can mend anything broke, 'cept my heart.'

'Then let me do that. For I will not go unless you come with me. Pa, we do not need to return to Alunby. I will take you away. Wherever you want to go, just name it.' Ben forced a smile; he had to make his father trust in him at least. 'You are my father. You are the man who brought me up and showed me how to be a man. You, and no one else.'

'Did you not hear what I said? Your father was Mathews. He admitted taking advantage of my Eleanor and he gave you the commission as a result to ease his conscience. I had been injured, he paid for my treatment, it saved my leg, but it cost me a good wife. She paid dearly! He acknowledged you as his son in recompense.' Joe was standing in front of him, his back straight for the first time.

'Perhaps he did, but he can never take my love away from you, which I hold for you and always will as a son. So come with me now and . . . and . . . ' Ben paled.

'What is it?' Joe asked.

'Teresa gave you the note. She knows she is my half sister . . . ' Ben backed away. 'I must leave now,' Ben's hand shook. The thoughts he had had, the dreams of this beautiful woman in his arms when she was his . . . ' He stared at Joe. 'We will leave Gorebeck. I will come for you tomorrow with a horse for you. We will ride to Whitby. From there we can make our plans. I will not lose you again,' Ben said softly. 'Where is the letter?' He reached for the coat, handed it to Joe who slipped it on. 'Do you have anything here you wish to take with us? If so, have it packed and ready for my return.'

Joe bent down and picked up his old bag of tools. It was as Ben remembered it, the only things which had stayed the same.

'Where is the letter, Pa? Did they take it off you?' Ben asked. 'I may have need of it.'

'No, they did not get the letter. For with it comes a birthright, which you may wish to challenge. You could be a very rich man, Ben.' Joe said, as he stepped out into the sunshine. 'I don't want a penny of it, though.'

'Neither do I, Pa. I don't need it, we are well provided for. I am a Captain and have been successful on the field as you taught me to be.' He placed his arm around his father's shoulders and walked him back across the garden and into the building. 'Take me to this letter!'

'That I won't do.' Joe stopped.

'Why? You said you had it still.'

Joe looked up at the sun. 'I said, they have not got it and that I will not return to Alunby. To retrieve it, you will have to.' Joe actually smiled. 'Will you return to me if you once have it?'

'Will the sun set tonight?' Ben asked.

'Aye, lad, it will.'

'Then I shall return. When did Teresa give it to you?'

'When she was a child, dreaming of treasure, only she had no idea what the treasure chest held. Still doesn't. Go home, think on it, where now, did I keep my baccy?'

Ben nodded. He hugged his father. 'I will return the day after tomorrow. Be ready for me and say your goodbyes here. You have no reason to feel shame or hide away. Father you will start to live again.'

Joe nodded. 'I will . . . son,' he added quietly, as he watched his boy leave him once more.

# 9

Teresa edged along a pew until she was almost hidden from sight by a tall stone pillar. She had made it into the church just in time, but Benjamin was not there. She stared at the stained glass window at the end of the church above the altar and prayed. She prayed she could find a way to escape the match her mother wished for. She prayed that Benjamin would become an important part of her life once more, and she prayed that her old friend Joe was well and would forgive her for her selfishness. Teresa did not even think of her treasure in her prayers, but she prayed that her mama would forgive her, one day, for going against her precious plans. She knew she had been a disappointment to her, but never understood why.

After what had only been about ten

minutes, but had seemed to Teresa like hours, she heard footsteps sounding upon the stone flagged floor of someone entering the church. She turned around and saw Benjamin striding boldly toward her.

She smiled broadly at him and was confused when he looked most seriously troubled, as he approached her.

'Ben, I have so much to tell you, that I do not know where to begin . . . '

He sat down next to her, giving the altar a cursory glance as he did so. 'And I you, Miss Teresa.'

'Ben, you must listen and, I hope, know what to do for I would act quickly. I am to be forced into a marriage I have no wish to endure. I have not met the man yet, but I believe he is a rogue and I do not want to meet him. I want to run away . . . with you somewhere . . . Will you help me?' She sounded as desperate as she felt. All her determination to be calm escaped her; the minute he came near she just wanted to be with him. He was a man

153

now, but the warmth her friendship with him had brought back to her was still there, magnified a hundred times it seemed to her. She was pleased that he seemed to relax as he settled next to her, although he was careful to keep a respectable space between them.

'Who is this man?' he asked. He was looking at his hat, which he held in his hand.

'Mr Brigton of Hewerton. He will inherit, only if he marries before his father dies. Do you know him?' She looked at him eagerly, hoping he would help her.

'I know of him. He is a man of the town. I have heard of his reputation. It is said that he disgraced a young woman of some standing. He is not for you. He was born to wealth . . . but then so were you. Tell me what you want of me, Teresa?' His face looked almost pained.

'I was brought up in the same tiny village that you were, Ben. Our homes differed but our days were often shared.

We enjoyed each other's company.' She smiled, but he did not. 'How is Joe?' she asked gently.

'He is better than I expected.'

'Can I see him, Ben?'

'Why?' Ben turned sideways so that one arm rested on the back of their pew the other one rested on the back of the pew in front.

'I wanted to know that he is well.' She looked at him, but he just stared back at her.

'And?'

'Oh, I gave him something before I left Alunby and I wondered if he still had it.' His eyes stared at her. Teresa did not know what to make of his expression. It seemed distant.

'What did you give him?'

Teresa hesitated. He raised an eyebrow. 'You will laugh at me.'

'I very much doubt that,' he replied calmly.

'A treasure.' Teresa blushed.

'What was the treasure, Teresa?' he persisted.

'I don't know. Your father buried it for me. I hoped to retrieve it as I think it holds family secrets and I think that somehow I must retrieve it. It may hold something that I should know. Mama tried to have me bury it, but I misunderstood. Instead I gave it to your pa to do it. Ben, I'm so sorry I left you and your pa, I had no choice, but I missed you dreadfully, please believe me.' She placed her hand gently on his knee. 'They told me I was going on a visit, not leaving. If I'd known, I would have run away then. I missed you so much.'

Instead of responding warmly as she had expected him to, he stepped away and replaced his hat upon his head. When they had met again his eyes seemed full of hope and what she thought had been . . . love. Now they were distant and she felt as though a cold breeze swept between them.

'I do believe you, Misty.' He swallowed. 'I have to travel to Alunby today. If you want to throw your reputation and marriage to the wind, then your solution is simple. Be ready within the hour.'

'How? What do I say to Mama?' Teresa spoke words that meant nothing to her for in her heart she did not care, but being faced with such an ultimatum at short notice gave her a moment of panic. The rush of excitement that swept through her told her it was what her heart desired more than anything else.

'It is your choice. A horse will be ready. One hour.' Without a further word he walked away.

★   ★   ★

Benjamin's pulsed raced. He hardly understood what he had done. If he did not stop her then he would be ruining the reputation of a woman who he could not marry — much as he desired to. What that made him he could not fathom. He was numbed to the core. Everything he had struggled to provide for, to match her family's wealth, to provide for his father, had been yanked abruptly from his grasp. If he had known the truth of it whilst he was in the prison, he may not have ever come out alive, for his heart would have been broken before his spirit ever would have. If his father's understanding was correct, he was her half-brother. What a mess.

Whatever the outcome, should she decide to stay or come with him, she was certainly going to lose the chance of marrying one of the biggest cads known to the region. The man was renowned for gaming, gambling and womanising. His father's wealth carried him. No wonder Brigton was determined to net himself an innocent wench, one not even aware of him. Well, half-sister or not, he was not going to have his Misty. Ben had made enough wealth from his time at war to see him, his father and her, whatever she was to him, right, if she decided to come. His head was struggling to grasp the magnitude of the events which were unfolding. Beneath it all he physically ached, his heart ached for a love he had nurtured and dreamed of for years, yet might well have to bury deep, like her treasure, only much, much deeper.

★   ★   ★

Teresa was wearing her travel coat. She had no riding outfit with her. She sat in the stone building, mesmerised by the stained glass window. What does she do next? If she returned to the house, she might disturb her mama. Yet she could hardly leave without a word or a note. What a mess, she thought. Her mind whirled at the possible ramifications of a hasty decision. Solemnly, she stood up as no inspiration came to her, but as she turned and walked along the pew to the aisle ready to leave, her eyes settled upon a smaller mural in the Lady Chapel. It was a depiction of a lamb. She smiled. 'I'll go, or I will never know what could have been.'

The house was very quiet. The maid was in the kitchen preparing dinner, no doubt, Teresa thought. Cynthia had not returned which made her task simpler. Teresa wrote a simple note to her mama.

'Dear Mama,

*I know this will be as a shock to you and will, no doubt, be yet another disappointment to you. However, I have taken the decision to return to Alunby, to see how uncle is, and will return tomorrow. I have a safe escort and if you can be calm, I shall be back before we are due to return to York. I shall then inform you what I have discovered and intend to do next.*

*Please find it in your heart to forgive me.*

*Your loving daughter,*
*Teresa.'*

She left the note on the pillow next to her mother's sleeping head and left.

Teresa waited by the archway. She felt anxiety sweeping through her body, but did not think that she could stand there too long. So, against her better judgement, she made her way to the stable block.

Benjamin was walking his horse out of its stall, saddled and ready to ride. He looked at her and half smiled.

'You decided to ruin your name then?' He walked up to her, his eyes softer than they had been. 'What is about to be done cannot be undone. Are you sure you can accept your destiny, Misty? This is no child's game. I too will be accused of stealing you away.'

'No, you will not for I have not implicated you at all. I have left a note only to say I return to Alunby to see my uncle. You have no part in this, nor Joe. I will make sure you are safe and beyond reproach.'

He shook his head slightly. 'Oh good,' he said dryly. 'You do not have a riding outfit with you?' he asked.

'No, I do not ride.' Teresa felt foolish for she had not thought to say that she had not sat astride a horse since he had taken her for gallops along the beach on his father's old horse.

He sighed. 'We had better make a swift start. We shall not need another horse.' Without further discussion he lifted her up onto the saddle then mounted the animal himself. She was seated sideways in front of him. He kicked the animal onwards and led the horse out through the archway and turned right to leave the town by the least public way. Hopefully, they would be unseen by the townsfolk or at least unnoticed by her mother's friend. As soon as they were in the cover of the woods beyond the town he stopped and let her slip down to the ground.

Teresa ached; sitting sideways like this was not at all comfortable, although she had the comfort of being able to hold him in her arms, which made it tolerable.

'You cannot travel that way. We will

never be there before dusk. Do you remember as a child how you sat astride the horse in front of me?' He had not dismounted.

'Yes, I do.' She was beaming at the happy memories, her eyes full of mischief just as they had been when she was a young girl.

'That is what you must do now, so that we may gallop.' He moved his foot out of the near stirrup and reached out his arm as he had done as a boy.

She would shamelessly bundle up her skirts to her knees, strain to put her foot in the empty stirrup and swing up and over the saddle so that she had been seated in front of him, but in those days she was a young girl. 'Ben, I can't, not now. It would not be proper.'

'Says the young maid who has just run away from her mama,' he quipped.

Deciding he had a valid point, she grabbed the hem of her skirts and bundled them up to her knees so that she could lift her leg high enough to swing her slight frame in front him. He watched her, his expression impassive, but the feel of the strength of the arm he wrapped around her waist filled her with a great sense of security, warmth and joy. He walked the horse back to the open track and without a word headed at speed for their old home of Alunby. With the wind on her face, pulling at her hair and bonnet, and the speed of the animal beneath them her senses were raw. The excitement mingled with exhilaration, she was not a child anymore, the sensations were very different, but she wished with all her heart they could keep going, just the two of them and never look back. This was happiness . . . this was bliss. Nothing, she thought, could surpass the sense of freedom she was now experiencing. All too soon the coast came into view and they had to slow the pace down. Instead of riding along the road, which would take them into the village by Marsh Farm Hall, he took an old track which led between fields and down to the dunes and the sandy beach beyond. They enjoyed a quick gallop along the flat sand, before he turned the horse's head to walk it back up to the rear of the old cottages, where he and his pa had once lived.

'You will need a spade,' Teresa said, a feeling of excitement still lingering as she thought of her quest and how the treasure would soon be revealed, whatever secret it held.

'I think not,' he commented, as they stopped behind the cottages, securing the horse to the old lean to.

He gently let Teresa slip to the ground first before he swung down. 'Yes you will because it is buried there . . . ' Teresa in her enthusiasm had rounded the corner of the old building to see the new building of the hall. The old workroom had gone, the stables rebuilt, in brick, over her designated spot. Her treasure was beyond her after everything she had done. Her future ruined, her mama furious, and her life's dream, the secret, never to be revealed to her. The arm she had used to point had frozen in mid-air before dropping to her side.

Ben stood at her side. She leaned gently against him. He placed an arm around her shoulders.

'Ben, it's all changed.'

'Things do, Teresa. We can't be children all our lives. The farm has grown, as have we.'

She struggled to hold back tears. 'I will never know what secrets it held. I have brought you here on a fool's errand and now we are both in trouble. Not children's trouble, Ben, but serious grown up trouble. I'm so sorry.' She saw his lip curl up at one corner in a faint smile.

'You did not bring me here, Misty. Cruelly and selfishly I brought you here to share a hurt. It was beneath me and it was selfish. I have destroyed your name in order to appease an anger, which is not and never could be borne against you . . . '

His words were interrupted by her sudden impetuous need to hold him, to hug him and be embraced in return. She flung her arms around him and held him close. Instead of responding in kind, as she thought her Ben would, he let out a long controlled sigh and patted her back awkwardly with his right hand.

'Misty, come with me . . . ' His voice broke, as if he was choking back his own emotions. Teresa did not understand why. Then a fear crossed her mind and stabbed at her heart — he was a married man. Of course! It made perfect sense. He had moved to the town with his wife and pa! He had said that they had their lives to lead also. What a fool she was! What a child!

He took hold of her hand and led her around the back of their old cottage. The townsfolk were busy inside their homes as the daylight had closed in.

Quietly, he took her to the place where his pa used to smoke his pipe, sitting peacefully upon his stool, watching the world go by, as he would say, when he was not busy. Ben took a small chisel from his pocket and started scratching around the edge of one of the bricks which made up this special place. It did not take long before the build up of earth and sand was removed and the loose brick was lifted. There, wrapped in a piece of seal skin was a tin box, black with a gold coloured edge.

Teresa's eyes widened. 'My treasure . . . He kept it safe!'

Ben just nodded, pocketed it, and walked back to the horse.

# 10

Teresa followed Ben to the back of the church. Here the old vicarage still nestled in its shadow. This was one part of the town which had not changed. Carefully, he tethered the horse under a tree and then, holding the tin in one hand and Teresa's hand in his other, he led her to the back of the church building. Teresa looked around her. Shadows seemed to dance amongst the gravestones, mocking her, as she shivered with cold anticipation, excitement and fear all mingled together into one explosive mass of feelings, which she could hardly contain.

Ben lifted the latch easily, there was no need to lock doors in this place as everybody knew everybody else and strangers were rare. He let them inside. He was quick to shut the door against the cool evening air and lead her into the vestry. Here he found a lamp, and used his flint to light it.

In the flicker of its glow, he set the tin box upon the oak table top and stepped backwards.

'It is your precious treasure, Teresa. If you wish to know the secrets it withholds, now is the time to find out.'

Teresa could hear his voice; she thought that he too was excited for it was not as calm as it had been. She stood by the table and looked down upon it. Her memory had played tricks upon her. She had imagined the tin box to be bigger, brighter and heavier. In fact, she could see now that it was no more than just an old tin, with no special redeeming features at all. Her mama was quite correct. If she had done as she had been told to when the woman was too ill to dispose of its contents herself, it would have rotted away. Long forgotten or lost.

'Why wait? Is it not your greatest desire, Misty, to know what is within it?' Ben said calmly and leaned over toward her as if willing her on.

'Not anymore.' Her reply surprised her, as much as it did him, apparently, for the lamp wavered in his grip and the light failed momentarily as it flickered within.

'Then before you tell me what your greatest desire is, open it and discover its contents.'

'You already know what is inside, Ben, don't you. Joe hid it, but he had opened it, hadn't he? Is that how you got your commission as a lieutenant?' She did not wish to insult his father, but she had had time to think about events.

'He was curious. He looked. Forgive him for the weakness of his humanity, but do not accuse him of being a thief, Misty, it is beneath both you and him. Now open it.'

She looked at him for a moment, still undecided. 'Do you have a wife, Ben?' she asked, and laughed as he nearly dropped the lamp.

'What! Me? No!'

'I seem to be wrong about so many things.' His reaction had dismissed her fears, so feeling the time was rife Teresa reached for the tin and lifted the lid. Wrapped in a piece of tanned skin, lined with cloth were two folded papers. The first one, Teresa lifted carefully toward the lamp. This had been secured by a wax seal, which had long since been broken. It had been sent to her mama from France.

Teresa's hands began to tremble as she read it. 'You know what this says?' she asked him.

He placed the lamp on the table and he reached out for it. 'I know what my father was told it said, that your father and mine are the same. Let me read it for my own peace of mind, if it will ever be possible for me to have peace again.'

'If that is true, then we can never be . . . ' Teresa's voice trailed off. She stifled her sob as she reached for the second piece of folded paper, trying to understand why her life was to be filled with this new travesty at a time when

172

she had at last found happiness. How could they ever exist together, in the same place, when they felt so attracted to each other if there was a tie of blood between them? Without words being spoken they exchanged knowing glances, understanding the other's pain.

Teresa took a deep breath and unfolded the second document. She wiped her tears from her eyes as she focused upon the words. It took a moment for her to make sense of what she held within her grasp. Why would her mama hide a notification of her father's death? But then she supposed the knowledge of her father's betrayal was too much of a burden for her to bear. It was too cruel. No wonder her mama was such a bitter woman. She had lost the love of her husband and then his life had been taken from her. Pity and disappointment overwhelmed her, until she saw the date of the despatch and of the date of his death. Teresa looked up at Ben, whose crestfallen expression showed all she needed to know about his feelings for her as he dropped the letter onto the table.

She took in a deep breath. From curiosity she had been led to a point of despair, back through confusion to hope.

'You should keep that safe, Ben. You could make a legal claim for the hall farm with the confession from the Colonel. You are his illegitimate, but recognised son. No wonder Mama wanted to hide these away from Mrs Shellow and Mr Johnston. You have more rights, possibly, than he, certainly than his brother.'

He looked at her with doleful eyes. 'You think I need to fight for the Colonel's scraps.'

'The Hall Farm and the land that goes with it, Ben, is far from what anyone could call 'scraps'.

Ben stood tall. 'As far as I am concerned, I have a father and his name is Joe Lamb. He is the only one I have ever known and the only one I will ever need to.'

'Good, that will save a lot of bad feeling,' she said brightly.

'You do not seem to be very upset at the discovery of having a half-brother?' he snapped.

'I am not.'

Ben sighed. 'Forgive me, I have misunderstood you. I thought that we, our meeting and our friendship that there was a chance that you felt the same way as I have done. But never mind ... I can see I have been quite wrong.' He cleared his throat. 'I will leave you with your uncle, and then tomorrow I will send word where you are to your mother, or return you safely, as you wish. Then I must collect my 'father' as I have much to catch up on and a new home to establish for us both.

'Ben, are you not curious about this?' She held the notice out for him. 'Read it,' she insisted.

'It says that your father 'Colonel Solomon Redford Matthews died a heroic death during a skirmish with

175

enemy troops on the 20th January . . . '
He looked up at her in disbelief. 'When were you born?'

'I never saw my father, ever, Ben. I only ever knew the tales that Joe Lamb told me of him. My birth date is 10$^{th}$ December that same year, Benjamin. Therefore, I cannot be the colonel's child!'

Teresa spun around. 'This treasure is greater than I could ever have imagined. We are free of their bonds, Ben. Do you not see that whatever tragedy and sin they stained their marriage with, ours does not have to be so. She slipped, when she spoke about my father. She insisted I treat Mr Johnston as my father. Why else would he pay for me, why else would she want me out of the way, because, like Joe, who she despises, we both reminded her of a time when her loneliness and her despair brought her low. Ben, I feel pity in my heart for her, and I will go and tell her what I know, but you and I are no more related than Ida is to my uncle.'

She stepped close to him. This time she would not be the first to fling her arms around him, she hoped.

Ben leaned his head next to hers. He slipped both documents inside his coat pocket, blew out the lamp and she felt his arms encircle her waist drawing her to him in a way that made her feel he would never let her go.

'Ben,' she whispered, 'We are in a cold church, night is falling and . . . '

Her words were smothered by his lips as she succumbed to the warmth which enveloped their beings. When they parted, he removed his jacket and wrapped it around her shoulders.

'Here,' he said softly and held out his hand.

'What is it?' she asked as she offered her own open palm to accept the gift.

Ben dropped the crudely made comb he had wanted to give her when she had left his life.

'Treasure, made by a boy who was in love with a beautiful girl, who has filled his dreams ever since.'

She accepted it graciously. 'It is priceless.'

'There has been enough travesty within your parents' marriage, Teresa. We must return to Gorebeck, reassure my father and face your mother. Then we can make a fresh start, but I insist we also go to York. I would speak to Mr Johnston.'

'Ben, you should not. He is my father. He could have you arrested or something for kidnapping me. They will not take my word over his.' Teresa's joy was turning to panic.

'Why would he reject me as a suitor for you?'

Teresa did not know how to answer without being blunt. 'He knows you are of 'humble' origins, Ben. He has Mr Brigton lined up as a possible suitor for me. He will be very angry at what we have done.'

'Teresa . . . Misty, I am Captain Benjamin Lamb. I am a man with my own means. I will not inherit, but I can provide a good home and what is more we have the evidence to lay claim to this place, if we chose to, and to discredit your mama. I do not think he would risk either. He is a man who values his own reputation and would do anything to protect the woman he loves, your mama. Father said they were alone together, running this place for years. Love strikes the best of us when we least expect it, Misty. I have loved you for years.'

He led her out into the moonlight. She turned the comb over in her fingers. 'Funny, Benjamin, all those years I dreamed of returning here to find my treasure and my future. It was true, I did . . . I found you.'

## THE END

CHLOE'S FRIEND
A PHOENIX RISES
ABIGAIL MOOR:
THE DARKEST DAWN
DISCOVERING ELLIE
TRUTH, LOVE AND LIES
SOPHIE'S DREAM

*Other titles in the*
*Linford Romance Library:*

## JUST A MEMORY AWAY

## Moyra Tarling

In hospital, Alison Montgomery cannot remember her own name. She hears the doctors' hushed whispers — sees their worried glances, which speak of the dark secrets lying just beyond the locked shutters of her memory. Then they bring her the stranger who says he's her husband. But why can't she remember loving a man as compelling as Nicholas Montgomery? And yet the shadows in his eyes clearly reveal that there's something in their past better left forgotten . . .

# SECRETS IN THE SAND

## Jane Retallick

When Sarah Daniels moves to a sleepy Cornish village her neighbour, local handyman and champion surfer, Ben Trelawny is intrigued. He falls in love with her stunning looks and quirky ways — but who is this woman? Why does she lock herself in her cottage — and why she is so guarded? When Ben finally gets past Sarah's barriers, a national newspaper reporter arrives in the village. Sarah disappears, making a decision that puts her life and future in jeopardy.

# WITHOUT A SHADOW OF DOUBT

## Teresa Ashby

Margaret Harris's boss, Jack Stanton, disappears in suspicious circumstances. The police want to track him down, but Margaret believes in him and wants to help him prove his innocence. Meanwhile, Bill Colbourne wants to marry her, but, unsure of her feelings, she can't think of the future until she finds Jack. And, when she does meet with him in Spain, she finally has to admit to Bill that she can't marry him — it's Jack Stanton who she loves.

# LOVE OR NOTHING

## Jasmina Svenne

It seemed too good an opportunity to miss . . . Impoverished by her father's death, Kate Spenser has been forced to give up music lessons, despite her talent. So when the enigmatic pianist John Hawksley comes to stay with her wealthy neighbours, Kate cannot resist asking him to teach her. She was not to know Hawksley's abrupt manner would cause friction between them, nor that the manipulative Euphemia would set out to ensnare the one man who seemed resistant to her charms . . .